Drew Campbell is an ex-punk, ex-mod, ex-waiter,
ex-factory worker, ex-funeral parlour assistant, ex-folk
guitarist, ex-civil servant, ex-trade unionist, ex-unemployed,
ex-local history researcher, ex-scriptwriter, ex-training
centre manager, ex-video company director, ex-bankrupt,
ex-creative writing tutor, ex-homeless person and ex-careers
advice worker. He is now advising himself to make a living as
a writer.

Dead Letter House

www.11-9.co.uk

Dead Letter House
Drew Campbell

First published by

303a The Pentagon Centre
36 Washington Street
GLASGOW
G3 8AZ
Tel: 0141-204-1109
Fax: 0141-221-5363
E-mail: info@nwp.sol.co.uk
www.nwp.co.uk

11:9 is funded by the Scottish Arts
Council National Lottery Fund.
ISBN 1-903238-29 3

Typeset in Utopia
Designed by Mark Blackadder

Printed by WS Bookwell, Finland

This book is dedicated to
Alison

CONTENTS

1: HOGMANAY

Happy New Year. I mean, Happy fucking New Year.

This big drunk man tottered over towards me swaying like a bridge in a gale. Our eyes had met across the Square a few seconds earlier and, though I had looked everywhere but him ever since, he fixed me with that sap-seeking antennae only these guys have and headed towards me like a confused, but determined missile. I focused on the twinkling Christmas decorations: ringing bells and swinging holly fashioned from light, beatific Santa faces winking one eye then the other. I looked back and the missile was still headed my way. He stood in front of me for a nanosecond smiling stupidly and blinking back tears. Then he did it. Launched himself at me and *kissed* me. A slobbering, squelching, regurgitated fortified wine-flavoured smacker right on the mouth. It's a wonder I didn't drop dead from hepatitis on the spot.

'Happy New Year,' he blubbed, tears and snotters blinding him.

Aye. Happy fucking New Year. It's shaping up to be a real doozy for me and it's only five minutes old. He takes a swig from his brown paper bag then sticks it under my nose. Sweet 'n' pungent. I decline.

'Tha's a nice soot, son. Nice soot ...' he fingered my lapels. 'Ah yoosed too 'aff a soot liek tha' – log tibe ago ... ' Tears and snotters welled up again. A wee bubble appeared from his nose and inflated in time to the whine emitting from his trembling lips. 'Log tibe ago ...'

I tried to unpick his grip on my jacket but it was no good. The muscles on his fingers were bigger than those on my arms, and they were hairier too. What else could I expect. These fingers had transported him from branch to branch throughout his life, while the hardest labour my puny limbs had ever attempted was a 5,000 word essay on the

Enlightenment.

'I yoosed ta huv' a soot jus' like that...' I could see it coming. The eyes hardened, the grip tightened. 'Gie's yer soot.'

'Well, I'd like to – mate – but you know how it is ... January, below zero, frostbite, hypothermia – I'm kinda using it, know what I mean?'

'Gie's ma soot.'

Notice the subtle change. Not just in the possessive, but in the tone – from the plaintive to the imperative. I mentioned this to my sartorial soul mate without apparent effect.

'Gie's ma soot.'

'Take it – it's yours.' He stood back with a stupid, satisfied smile and I stood up, making like I was taking the jacket off. 'Nice night for it,' I said.

Your man staggered on the spot and took another swig. ' 'urriup.'

Fucking prick. Fucking stupid arsehole. He's already brain dead, so why not just step out into the traffic and finish the job. Go on, you fucking loser. Do it, do it.

I decide to give him a lead. I jump out and into the traffic, darting across and bringing a screech from five sets of brakes. Yes!

But Noddy doesn't follow me. He's wandering about, looking forlorn and guarding the bench I sat on. He didn't even see where I went and his antennae's got brewer's droop now.

Nevertheless this is typical of how my night's going. And all I want to do is get home.

2: NECROPOLIS

Such a face, such a face. So smooth and white and flawless. So innocent and wise and beautiful. Lovely little cherub nose and cheeks and lips ... lips that have never been kissed. Ah ... but no eyes. Just whites. Unseeing. An angel that's never seen the world and never been kissed. Maybe I could kiss her. Maybe I could be the first if I could just ...

If I could just make it across from ...   here ...
to ...

that ...

bit ...

there ...

HUP!!

Done it.

'TOP OF THE WORLD, MA!
TOP OF THE WORLD!'

Why do you suppose someone would want a big statue of an angel sat on top of a big oblong plinth sat on top of a big muckle granite block sat on top of their grave? And then stick an iron spike fence around it just to be sure? Were they afraid someone would try and rob their bones after they've been interred? Or maybe the folk they left behind were afraid they'd try and claw their way out one dark and stormy night.

Whoaaah. Watch it now. You don't want to be slipping on icy little ledges under your feet, casting you down to be impaled on rusty old iron spikes. No way. No thank you.

Okay. Nothing to worry about. Nothing to get upset about. We're fine. Hey – we're meant for better things. Immortal you and me. We're not going to stumble into a daft accident when the world is waiting for you to ... well, do whatever it is you're going to do with your life. But I know it'll be important, significant.

It must be. I can feel it. You can't cheat destiny, whatever it is. And whatever it is, it's not throwing your life away on a silly accident. Right?

Right.

This place is full of it. Full of monuments to long-dead people nobody remembers or cares about. But this angel ... ah, what a face, what a face. You remind me of someone. Someone waiting to be kissed.

I put my arm around her, and she's so cold, so cold. White-eyed stare unflinching, she ignores me.

'Listen, I just want to kiss you. We'll only go as far as you want to. I won't force you to do anything you don't want to.'

Not that I could. I wonder how long she's stood here, gazing sightlessly out at the dark mausoleum and the black skyline of the city beyond. Hm? One hundred years? Two hundred years? Hm? How long have you been waiting for a kiss to bring you to life? A gallant prince to awake you from your frozen slumber atop this cold, cold hillside? How long, my beautiful angel?

C'mon now. One little kiss. How much could it hurt?

'HEY!'

Fuck's sake! I nearly tumble off the plinth.

'HOI! What are you doin' up there?'

Fuck's sake! Fuckin' hell! Who the fuck is that?

'HO! What're you doin'?'

There's four of them standing at the bottom of the slope, just outside the perimeter wall. Talking loudly. Slugging wine out of the same bottle.

'HEY! What're you doin'?' says the fat one. He turns to his mates, 'Do you recognise him?'

'Ehm ... let's just go. This is weird. He might be a nutter.'

The big guy pipes up: 'Naaaah! Standing fifteen

feet up in a graveyard on Hogmanay givin' it big Frenchies to a statue? How could he be a nutter?'

They all laugh. Arseholes.

'Hey! C'mon down, man! You'll kill yourself up there!'

Not me, mate. I'm protected. I've got a destiny to fulfil. Why don't you just fuck off?

'C'mon, man. This is just a bad situation. Let's get out of here.'

Yeh. Listen to the wee man. Piss off.

'No, wait. I think I know him ... '

Wait a minute. I know that voice ...

'Hey, isn't he that guy you used to know from the uni?'

'What guy? There's only a thousand to choose from.'

'C'mon, man, let's go.'

'Shut up, Stan,' says the fat one, obviously the leader. He shouts up to me again. 'Um, Happy New Year an' that. What are you doin' up there?'

'Podge?' I say.

'Hey! He knows us!'

3: RED ROAD

Podge, Wilson, Boolie, Stan and me are walking up the Red Road and it's pitch black. There's some peelie-wally yellow lights which make me think I'm a bit sick but it feels better to be breathing fresh air and be in company again. They're a shower of dicks really, but it was either go with them or catch that last bus.

'So how did you get an invite to the party at the graveyard?'

I should've went home, I should've went home.

'Was that your bird you were winching up there, pal?'

Shut up, you fucking prick. God, what a bunch of arseholes. I should've got that last bus home. Come to think of it, I should never have left home this evening. It's just gone from bad to worse.

Remember. Vivienne's house. Big House. Big West End house. Her folks' house. You're going to see the New Year in there. Just a couple of drinks at the Bells then on to some hip party with her hip friends. Except you never get that far. You can't get out of her parents' house. They're all dressed to the nines. Talking about you. Whispering. And you look ridiculous. Red suede shoes – oh fuck! Jesus! The Taste Police should've lifted you. And that bastardarse laughing at you. **BAstard. ARse**. Happy New Year, he said. And it wasn't even 11 o' clock (tick, tock). Then …

… something happened. Somehow I pushed bastardarse into the bin and his mate thumped me one in the chest but it didn't hurt and

He was kissing Vivienne. Not just kissing – winching, feeling, groping. That's why! The prick! The fucking rugby club middle class **bastardarse prick**!

'What'd you say?'

Stan. Podge's pal. I remember him now. What a

diddy. What an absolute loser. It's going to be a doozy of a year if bringing it in with him and Podge and their stupid mates is anything to go by.

'Where is this place?' I enquire.

'Just up here,' says Podge.

Where's here? 'Where's here?'

'Here. The Red Road.'

'Doesn't look very red to me.'

'Naw – the Red Road. Christ! How long have you been going to Glasgow, man? Haven't you worked out any basic geography yet?'

'I don't do Geography. I do History and Philosophy.'

'Oooh. History and Philosophy. Get him.'

This is that big tit Wilson. I've met him before as well. In the Union Bar I think. He was there with Podge and Panny and someone else. I was with Vivienne, I think.

I wish I was with her now. I wish we were lying in that bed in her mate's flat, naked and together and curled up with a few good tapes and a bottle of cheap red plonk and we had just made love and I could smell her and touch her and we could be happy without laughing and tired without sleeping and together without having to worry about families and what her Dad might think of me and what my Dad might think of her Dad and all that shite. I wish that's where I was right now.

I wish I'd never went to that party. I knew it was a mistake. I knew all her fucking well-off, well-fed, well-heeled friends would just look down their noses at me, I just fucking knew it. And her mummy and daddy and fucking auntie and uncle and grannie and all the rest of them trying to make polite conversation with me but all the time their eyes are saying, 'you're not good enough for her. You're just a common little oik from nowhere.'

Keeping me talking. All the while that bastardarse is fucking luring her into the kitchen and putting his big fucking rugby player hands all over her and slobbering his big fucking chops all over her and they're still chatting away like they give a fuck about me or anything I have to say and they know he's in there with her and they're just praying that he'll ... and they know she's ... she's ...

'What the fuck are you muttering about, man?'

Podge. He was a right swot at school. We weren't really friends but we were the only two to go to university from our school – probably ever – so we kind of hung about together in the first year. Shared the bus in in the mornings. Then he got a flat in town. Asked me if I wanted in on it. I should've. I wish I had. Then again these are probably his flatmates.

'Are you alright? What's up with you?

'Nothin',' says I.

Nothing. Right. No-thing. It was the look she gave me. The way they casually separated when I walked into the kitchen. She looked straight past me. Face impassive. Eyes trying to conceal ... trying to suppress ...

... that look of ... of ...

TRIUMPH. Triumph. That's what it was. When I lamped the guy and he tumbled into the pedal bin. That feeling she was vindicated, that I'd reverted to type. A working-class, ill-mannered oik, university place or no university place.

'This is it.' Podge says, stater of the fucking obvious. He's pointing to a giant concrete block with tiny wee rectangles of light all over it. It must be a thousand feet high. It leans over and has a quick shufty at us five at its feet, then set itself upright again.

Oh fuck. I hope it's on the first floor. Anything less than five, just please.

'It's the top floor.'

Podge – you're a prick.

The five of us cram in to the lift. That guy Boolie is a bit rank. At least I think it's him. Probably none of them wash in that flat of theirs. It's certainly not me anyway.

'It's not working, I bet it's not working.' This guy Stan's a real Cassandra.

'Shut up, Stan. Press the fucking button.'

To our surprise, it judders into action. The doors strain to close together, emitting a screechy wee whine to let us know how much of an effort this is going to be. Then it pitches a semitone higher as it climbs the long dark shaft.

We watch the lights.

Somebody coughs.

We watch the lights.

It smells like someone died in here.

We watch the lights.

This is going to take forever.

We watch the lights.

Somebody farts.

I'm about to make a jokey remark but everyone else pretends not to notice. Jesus! It's a bad day when you can't even make a joke about your mate farting in a lift! Not that they're my mates, but they're supposed to be mates with each other. I think.

We watch the lights.

I can't breathe.

We watch the lights.

If this thing stops we're dead.

We watch the lights.

There's too much weight. It's going to break down. I can feel it.

We watch the lights.

Jesus! I've got to get out of here! I'm choking! I can't breathe! I'm suffocating! I'm …

The lift doors open and we fall out onto the landing, panting and gasping and choking. My lungs are torched, my eyes are running and I'm sweating buckets. I lay on the floor feeling the 30-odd floors below me throbbing and ebbing away. This floor was cool and hard and dirty, but I lay my face against it and it soothed me.

(Maybe she was right. Maybe I am just a ...)
I'm alright now.
I'm alright.
Right.

4: PARTY

A suspicious pair of eyes keeked round the shard of space left by the barely opened door. I say a pair of eyes – there were two of them but they barely matched. They seemed to be sussing out all of us but each eye acted more or less independently of the other.

'Whit?' the door rasped like it was talking through its letterbox.

'Hi, man,' said Podge. 'Happy New Year n'that. We were just wonderin' if you had any blow goin', y'know.'

The eyes scanned him warily. Podge offered credentials. 'I'm Stuart. I go to the Uni. I've bought some stuff off of you at the Union a couple of times.' No response. 'Panny introduced us.'

'Show us money,' ordered the door. It had obviously seen better days. It had been a pale, insipid Corporation-standard yellow in its heyday but a few centuries of graffiti showed it was past this first flush of youth, and at least one attempt to burn it down was evidenced by a brown and black scar the length of its open side. Podge continued negotiations with the door. For some reason this struck me as biblical and I struggled to recall the bit it brought to mind.

'Is this biblical? This is biblical,' I whispered to Wilson.

'More like *Life of Brian*.'

The door stood aside and we entered the inner sanctum, at least the outer bit of it. We single filed down an incredibly long, dark, narrow hall with me, myself, bringing up the rear. I couldn't see anything except a smoky yellow light filtering through the cracks in (another) door at the end of this tunnel. Dank noise and music and talk buffled behind it and I touched the walls to steady myself. They were moist, bereft of paper. The floor was bare boards. Very Habitat. Very

'Modern Homes' colour supplement.

You know the bit at the end of *Raiders of the Lost Ark* where they open the Ark and these crazy, ethereal spirits jump out, well, it was a bit like that. Hash smoke burst out, flew up the hall to greet us, and we're all going '... is beeyooteefull, is beeyooteefull' like the French guy, and then it jumps down your throat and chokes you. At the same time 10,000 ZappaWatts cannoned at us, but fortunately Podge's bulk absorbed the major impact.

We five filed in like we were leg-ironed together. I knew I would stand out as all the others were in denim and khaki, whereas I had plumped for a silvery grey suit and a Picasso-on-acid kipper tie. Oh, and red suede shoes. Lest we forget.

Podge and the lads kept their heads down and headed for the kitchen – they might have been whistling *Colonel Bogey* but I couldn't hear over Mad Frank's decibels – but I stopped and scanned the room. Bikers. Hundreds of them. Oh shit.

It was like walking into soup. Some people swirled around in the middle, some individuals bounced off the walls, and some lay in little lumps and clusters at the bottom of the pot. The air was thick and damp, bodies slouched in every orifice and the smell of sweat and leather could curl your toenails. A topless chick had her hand down the front of this big guy's jeans and was chewing his face and neck like she hadn't seen food for a week. Her straight brown hair went all the way down to her arse and her split ends did an incredible dance at the top of her tight denim thighs as she squirmed and shimmied over this guy's torso. She had elliptical, red brown nipples on small, white breasts and as my eyes fixed on them the guy's mouth came down and swallowed one of them whole.

I blinked away. Nobody else was even watching them. Groups of two and three leathers and denims huddled together over bongs or pipes or joints and nodded their heads as Zappa bludgeoned on. I seriously considered adjourning to the toilet to relieve my inflamed underpants but a hand felt my shoulder and I nearly jumped out the window.

'Money, man.'

It was Wilson. I followed him into the kitchen grateful for the excuse to fumble in my pockets and cover my obvious embarrassment, now receding by the second. There were about fourteen people in this tiny kitchenette, but Podge and The Voice & Eyes Of The Door were shoehorned into chairettes at a little tablette.

The Voice & Eyes Of The Door followed me into the room with one eye, while his other concentrated on the cutting and weighing exercise at his fingertips.

'Yer 12 pounds light.'

Incredibly, this was aimed at Podge. Podge beckoned me to sit down. There being no more chairettes, I pulled up my hunkers and sat on them.

'He said you're 12 pounds light, Podge. I'd check the cut he gives us because he obviously can't judge weights.'

'Shut up, you tit. He means pounds sterling. How much have you got?'

'Well, I haven't got 12 pounds to spare.'

'Shit, man. Give us your dosh.'

Now, I stood up to get my money out of my incredibly tight trousers and paused. There's no way I'm chipping any more than a tenner into this deal, but I've got about 22 quid on me and it's all rolled up together. And if I show, there'll be no getting out of it after that.

'How much are we getting?'

The Voice & Eyes stopped footering with his hash and scales. He was an evil looking git. Jaundiced skin climbed up on a scrawny neck from his black T-shirt, shoulders dappled with a blizzard of dandruff. The beginnings of jowls fetched down around his chin and jaws as one eye focused on the fag he was rolling and the other on me. A brown tongue darted out and sealed the spine of the fag, then promptly pulled into the thin, ochre lips of a cruel, nervous mouth. As he lit it, the lips drew back to reveal twisted teeth, each as jaundiced and yellow as his skin, and all chipped and gapped on brown receding gums. Grey and white stubble littered the bottom half of the face, dissected on the left side by a scar running from the corner of the mouth almost to the temple. The tip of an off-centre snout-nose protruded aggressively in the middle. Above it, the ridge was almost flat to the face like a clay model sculptor had pressed his thumb on it. His hair was short, black and wispy, contriving to make the best of early balding, and I got the feeling he fancied himself as a bit of a Jack Nicholson type. However, in this feeble attempt he was defeated by the eyes. One was small, piggy, shifty and black, and the other was large, stretched, lazy and brown. The overall effect was of a drawing discarded by an eleven year old who hadn't quite mastered proportions. His voice was, I think, naturally quite high, but years of smoking and trying to sound tough gave him an odd, whiny rasp.

'See?' He held up a tiny pebble of hash between his thumb and forefinger.

'And how much are we paying for that?'

Podge answered for him. 'It's a sixty quid deal, man. Twelve each. Fair's fair. Cough up.'

'A sixty quid deal? Is that really necessary, Podge? I mean, I don't see you guys too often and I don't see us getting through 60 quid's worth tonight, do you?' Note the irony in my voice.

Podge leaned over and hissed: 'Jakesie's getting impatient, man. It's a 60 quid deal. Cough up.'

'Oh, Jakesie's getting' impatient, is he?' I just whispered this bit to Podge but Jakesie's lazy eye could probably lip read. 'Look, Jakesie – can I call you Jakesie? Jakesie. We're just out for a wee blow on Hogmanay. I know we should've prepared better, but we didn't. We're really only looking for a 40 pound deal – what d'you say? Hm?' I turned to Wilson and the others who were all drawing me daggers. 'A 40 quid deal – eh? Isn't that better. Eight quid each. Jakesie gives each of you … ehm … two quid back, then I give you all two quid. What d'you say?'

Wilson was beetroot. Boolie looked at his shoes and Stan just looked blank. Podge turned to Jakesie. 'Could me and my compadres have a little word in private, somewhere … please? Jakesie?'

'Sure.' He grinned. He actually grinned. It was more plaque than teeth but he did grin. In the fridge behind me a pint of milk curdled.

Wilson and Podge practically frogmarched me through the living-room – whose incumbents all looked half dead – and found a relatively uninhabited corner. The four crowded around me. I keeked past Wilson's large meaty shoulder to see if I could see the topless dancer again but she was gone. Then they pushed me into the hall and closed the door.

'What's with you, you prick?'

'Don't fuck with a guy like Jakesie!'

'C'mon, man. This is a pure neck. We're losin' face badly here.'

'Jakesie's seriously put out.'

'He doesn't seem that bothered to me.'

'What fucking planet are you on?'

'You're fucking with him!'

'I'm not fucking with him, I'm just trying to get things sorted properly.'

'You're the one who's gonna get sorted properly!'

'By you, I suppose.'

'Oh, God. This is seriously heavy. We are seriously losing face here.'

'Fuck up, Stan. Stop saying that.'

'Look. It's very simple. The guy is ripping us off. That deal is never worth sixty quid. No way.'

'You don't understand, man. You're such a fucking prick!'

'I do understand. We've come in, we've disturbed the guy's party to do a deal and he's bumped up the price. He's ripping us off.'

'That's not the point!'

'It is the point. We take a forty quid deal – which will still be a rip off, but at least it's what we agreed in the first place – then stick around for an hour or so and sponge off the dope going round here. The place is hoochin' with it. That way, we make up some of the difference and … '

'Are you for real?'

'Are you fucking serious? These guys are mental. I just want to do the deal and get out. And we're supposed to be going to Alan Kilgour's – remember?'

'Listen, this is a wild party, and it's going to get wilder. I think we should stay with it and … '

'He's certifiable. I'm off.'

'Let's go back to Jakesie and plead for mercy.'

'Oh, God. What a neck. What humiliation. What a loss of … '

'Will you shut the fuck up, Stan!'

They leave me in the hall. I shrug. Fuck them.

Fuck them.

I traipse back through to the kitchenette after them.

5: THE DEAL

'Sixty quid, please, gents.' Jakesie was almost laughing now.

'Ehm … Jakesie?' Podge hesitated. 'This looks a wee bit smaller than what we were, eh, discussing a moment ago.'

'No. Not a moment ago. Many moments ago. A thousand, maybe a million, moments have passed since we spoke and time is money – understand?' Jakesie's face instantaneously atrophied into a fearsome mask and stayed that way while a few million more moments passed. Podge reddened and sweated.

'Yeh … uh … yeh. I suppose. Sorry.' He handed over 60 quid.

Wilson managed to speak. 'Um … well, we'll be off then. Enjoy your party.'

'Have a nice new year Mr … ehm … Jakesie.' That was Stan. Wilson pushed him out of the door. Podge and Boolie followed. They went straight through the living-room, through the hall and out the door without looking up.

I was left.

6: WAGGING TONGUES

My head starts to spin. I feel queasy. My tongue starts to vibrate in my mouth though, for once, I'm not speaking. Just blethering in my head. Like this.

This tongue is taking on a life of its own. It's thin and wriggly like a worm, like a worm, maybe it's a worm slithering and stretching all the way up from my stomach and through my intestine and my oesophagus and my trachea and God i'm going to be seeeeck i'm going to be sooooooo seeeeck and this worm's going to pop out and … and … (why am i thinking so little? everythink i thing is wee) … It's getting bigger. I Mean Bigger! It's THICK and **JUICY** and maybe and maybe and maybe and maybe I could just bite into it like a big steak.

NO! Stoppit, fucking stoppit.

I don't think it's attached to me any more. It's not a worm it's a … A big slow fat SNAil … crawling up from my bowels licking and oozing around all the caverns of my mouth, my throat, my head – NO!! Stoppit. Just fucking stoppit.

Fucking stoppit. Get a grip. Fucking tongue – it's a drill now (no it's not). **Drrrrrrrrrrrr Drrrrrrrrrrrrr Drrrrrrrrrrrrrrrr Drrrrrrrrrrrrrrrrr**rilling through my teeth! Ah! Aaaaaaaaaaaagugh!

I whack my head off   (**SOMETHING – ing – ing – ing!!!**)   then rest my head against its coolness. Whoa. Chill out, chill out. Cool. Cold. Soothing. Soothe me.

What's happening to me? Get a grip. Think. I'm with Vivienne. She's my …

no. No, she's not.

(my scalp is crawling … getting tight and cold …) She's … we're … (oh, fuck! the skin is crawling off my head) ooooohhhhhhh...

I whack my head off the … (   ) again.

It shakes.

Beach. Find a beach. I'll be alright on a beach.

Right.

Stoppit.

It's cool. Everything's cool. (it's cold but i'm fucking sweating.) No, it's cool.

She must've been about 30, but what a bod. I couldn't see her face at first. I was lying in a stoned heap behind the hi-fi speakers where it was quiet.

'Do you want to dance?'

My head raised by degrees, minutes, or seconds even. It was so heavy. My face was so light but my head was so heavy.

'Do you want to dance?'

My eyelids ratcheted open and confused pupils squinted towards the voice. A naked light bulb glared back and a hand came up and shielded the eyes. Then a beautiful black silhouette eclipsed the light and stood there, rocking gently in time to the music.

I didn't recognise the song now – the tirade thudding through my head when I lay down here was gone, thank Christ. Now there was this swaying, sexy, seductive rhythm and subtle, sensuous, sensual beat. And this sashaying silhouette.

'Do you want to dance?'

'Do I … ? Yes. Yes, of course.'

I stood up – too fast. My head was still supine as my feet reached the floor. I pulled at my face and it felt like I was ploughing through cold, grey clay. Shake head. Oh, bad idea. I'm all over the place. Get a grip, get a grip, get a grip. Right. Now. Check it.

I realise somehow I've lost my suit but it's cool 'cos – Whoah! A black leather biker's jacket. Still got the red suedes though.

My crotch feels a bit sweaty so I check I haven't pissed myself as nonchalantly as poss. No problem. No problemo.

Why am I thinking like this? Why am I dressed like this?

'Do you want to dance?'

Fuck me, she's beginning to sound like a broken record. Didn't I just answer her? No, mebbe not.

Right then.

'Yeh. Yeh. Let's dance.'

I move into the middle of the floor, stepping over a couple of sleeping corpses. In fact, everyone seems to be asleep.

She links her hands behind my neck keeping me at arm's length and turning me round so I see her face. She is gorgeous. Thick, black hair in a heavy fringe cut square down to her shoulders. Large dark eyes, round and sexy, with thick, black, coated lashes dropping a veil across when I look too deeply. My hands rest on her hips and then move to her waist. She takes a deep breath. I move them back to her hips and she smiles. Large, white teeth and thick red lips. She pouts. God. I'm in heaven.

We move a little closer and I feel the leather covering her crotch rub against the inside of my thigh. Jesus. I want to look down, but her eyes are staring into mine, like she's transmitting some telepathic song. I drink her in.

She's wearing a tight, ribbed black sweater that stops on her midriff, and a smooth white belly peeks out from the top of her high, black leather jeans. My hands touch the exposed skin and I gently pull her closer still. The pulse is more insistent now, building and building as we join at the hip and move hard together in time to the beat – bumping, teasing, tightening, squeezing beat. My right hand slides under her thigh, along the leather and down to her knee, pulling it up so her calf and heel grips my backside with her high heeled boots. My left hand fingers ripple across the ribs of her sweater and over the outline of her left breast. Her nipple rises beneath the tight stitches in response. She arches her back, lets her head fall back with it and lets me take her full weight as she slowly swings her hair from side to side. Her neck, her throat, are naked, exposed. I push the back of her head towards me slightly and kiss the soft, white skin. Her fragrance is hot, human, real. I want her. I want her now.

Our mouths meet – tenderly at first then, as I taste the full, pulsating passion in her lips, wildly, madly, to death. Her tongue caresses mine, tugging urgently, desperately. I run my hand through her hair, feeling its warmth playing with my fingers and palm.

Suddenly she pulls the back of my hair – hard, sharply. My eyes burn and I glare into her eyes – pensive but … laughing. She relaxes her grip and kisses my eyelids, my nose, my cheeks.

'Take me away.'

Where? Where could I take her? Where can I go?

'Where? Where do you want to go?'

'Take me. Away.'

We stand, still embracing, but staring into each other's eyes. My heart thumps against her breast, her heart thumps into my chest. I kiss her gently, take her hand, and lead her towards the hall.

It is still dark and bare in the hall. Our footsteps echo on the floorboards and our breathing on the walls and ceiling. We go to a bedroom. It's busy. We go to the other bedroom. Even busier, but she walks in like she owns the place. The couple on the bed are really going for it and appear not to notice our entrance.

'Here – take this.' She throws a hold-all at me. It's full of clothes, make-up, costume jewellery, musty paperbacks and cheap trinkets, and it weighs a ton.

'Where are we going?'

'Just take me away.'

This isn't quite the deal I thought it was. She seems impatient, angry even and I'm not sure what's happening. On the bed the girl moves on top and starts riding this guy like her life depends on it, completely oblivious of our little drama three feet away.

'Take me away now!'

I want to, I really do, but … I can't take my eyes off this couple. They are both naked, but so wrapped in each other, so much in love, they can't see anything but each other. The girl's frenetic ride slows down but now they are moving as one. And you can see the tension – a hard, exquisite tension – spread through their bodies and turn them into one, complete being. The girl seems almost to stop, but her movements have become minuscule, almost imperceptible. Her breaths are actually tiny screams, pitched just above the range of human hearing. Then a flood swells through them, raising them skywards for a second, then washing them up on some lonely, distant beach.

I realise She is right next to me, gripping my arm so tightly it hurts. She hisses into my ear: 'Take. Me. Away. Now.'

I look at her. Her eyes are wide, maybe slightly glassy. I have to have her now. I have to have her now. I grab her hand and pull her out of the door, across the hall and into the toilet.

I pull the cord inside the door and a harsh, white light bursts brightly onto more whiteness. Everything is white. White light, white walls, white toilet, white bath, white ceiling. There's no window. Instead a fan blasts on whirring loudly and blocking everything, every sound outside, as I close the door and seal us in the whiteness. She stands with her back to the door, facing me. I scan the contours of her black sweater and black leather jeans, relieving the tyranny of the light, seeing her breasts and the swell below her waistline pant and rise and pant and rise and pant and rise. I raise my eyes, look at her long neck, her soft, black hair, her full, red lips, her round, dark, dark eyes. Her eyes.

Her eyes. She seems … irritated. Annoyed, even.

'Not here. Take me away.'

'What? I … '

'Take me away. I've got to get away. Take me away.'

'But I … I want you. Now. I've got to.'

Her brows knotted and she frowned. I kissed her mouth, but she didn't kiss back.

'What's wrong? I thought you … wanted to.'

'I do. Not here. Take me away.'

'Please. I've got to. I've got to now.'

She sighed impatiently. 'Oh … right, right. OK. But be quick. OK?'

' … Yes. Sure.'

'And afterwards – take me away, OK?'

'Yes, yes. Anything.'

Then she kissed me – suddenly, and hard. She held my face against hers and sucked and pressed and licked my mouth while I undid my trousers and fumbled for her zip. She let go of me for a minute and undid it herself, slipping out of one leg and letting them fall to the floor. In the same movement she wriggled out of one leg of her knickers and let them fall too.

Her long, white thighs were so smooth, so beautiful, I wanted to kiss them. She was holding my neck tightly but I squeezed down between her arms and kissed her soft, fleshy belly, sticking my tongue into her belly button. Her hands moved down too and tugged my hair, but I kept moving down. I traced the line at the top of her thighs and along her groin, letting my face brush the thick, black crop of hair at her cunt. I started to nestle my nose into its thick warmth, letting my hands stroke up and down the back of her legs. Suddenly she gripped my hair hard and pulled me up to her face, forcing my hips against hers.

'Fuck me,' she said. 'Fuck me right now.'

My cock was wet and tall, covered in that clear, pre-coital silk as I pushed it under her thick, bushy hair and into her lips. She was a little dry but I slipped inside her without too much trouble.

I thought my head was going to lift off. I could feel her soft muscle gently resisting me, then as I pushed a few strokes, I felt her pull away inside and a large, wet cavern open up. It was hard to move where we were standing – the floor was slippy and I couldn't get any purchase on it to thrust. She was wriggling around on me and still sucking at my face and neck. I tried to grip the cheeks of her backside but I nearly fell. She was acting wild, crazy, like an animal, but I was just trying to stay upright. I pushed hard against the door and it started rattling in time to our thrusts, but at least I could get going.

'Hurry up,' she whispered urgently, bearing down on me. 'Hurry up.'

I redoubled my efforts but my left leg gave way and we both nearly tumbled into the wash-hand basin. We pushed ourselves upright again and I tried to get the rhythm back but she was fidgeting and trying to re-position herself. I pushed in again. I pulled up her sweater to reveal her left breast and craned my neck to try and tease her nipple, but it was flaccid and flat so I sucked her whole tit instead.

She pulled my head up again. 'Come on, come on. Come now.'

I was nowhere near it. No way. In fact I felt very tired and sore and a bit fed up.

'Come on! Come now!' she said out loud.

I tried harder. I went hell for leather, drilling in as fast as I could. The door thumped and rattled and creaked and banged in time with our – my – fucking, and the drone of the fan whirred and burned and turned and thudded in my brain. I wanted to come. I tried to come. But I couldn't. I just couldn't.

'What's the matter with you? Why don't you come?' she moaned.

'I … I … I … I …'

I stopped.

'I'm sorry.'

8: VIOLENCE

But the door kept on banging and thudding. Shut up! Shut up! We've stopped!

But the door kept on banging. Then it started mewling and howling and she went crazy.

But the door kept on banging. Then it started seething and cursing like a mad beast and she pushed me onto the floor and frantically pulled up her knickers and her leather jeans and pulled down her black ribbed sweater and stood back from the door for fear of it and she shook with terror and started blubbering and whimpering and thick black tears ran down her face, like the colour running from her eyes and she's staring at the door and the door's bulging and throbbing and bending towards her like it's trying to jump off its hinges and wrap itself around her.

I'm scrabbling about on the floor, knowing something's going to happen – but what? What? What've I done?

The lock flies off the door and Jakesie bursts in and kicks her viciously in the stomach. I …

fell back into the bath. And watched. Shaking. Shitting myself. He punched her … he punched her like he was punching a man – again and again and again. In her face, in her throat, on her breasts, on her ribs. And kicking her – on her thighs, in her crotch. And she's coughing and choking and boaking and a lump of bloody mucus shoots out of her mouth and on to his forearm and he screeches with rage like she spat at him on purpose and he grabs her by the hair and swings her head into the wash-hand basin. And she groans like she's nearly unconscious but he hauls her up and screams at her – fuckfuckfuckfuckfuckfuckfuckingcow! fuckfuckfuckfuckfuckfuckfuckingwhore! bitch! cow-whore! cow-whore-bitch! – then he hauls her up to her feet and SMASHES!!! God! He … smash … shhhh … shh … shh

... sh ... ed ... her ... f ... f ... f-f-f-face. Into. the. mirror.

Screeeeeeaaaams!! She screeeeeeeaaaaams! And it cracks the glass and it splinters and there's hundreds of fractured reflections screaming back at her and hundreds of jagged Jakesies hissing and seething into her ear for eternity and he's muttering something. I didn't know then but I know now what he said. He said:

'Remember this moment forever.'

Then he pulls a long, sharp shard from the mirror and ... cuts. Red Blood Pours from her, spews, floods from her face ... her skin ... her skin. Oh God. Ohgod ohfuck ohgod. I'm...

her skin. No. Oh no no no no no no no no no no no no no. She's dying ... she's on the white-red floor ... she's ... I'm retching ... I'm sick, I'm suh ... suh ... I'm ...

'You, you fuckin' little cunt!'

Jakesie faces me, a jagged bloody blade of glass in his hand.

9: FLIGHT(S)

I can fly.
I haven't quite mastered it yet, though.
I just flew down 8 sets of stairs,
and each set has 12 stairs in it,

so that's 96 stairs in all.
Call it 100.
It's incredible.
But credit where it's due.
Jakesie helped.

He threw me down the first set. I touched down heavily on the landing but rolled back onto my feet and propped my back against the wall. At first, I was amazed to be alive. My eyebrow, cheekbone, shoulder and the palms of my hands were bleeding, though not too badly I think. My head caught up with the rest of me and I focused on the hellish vision above me.

Jakesie could fly too, it seemed, and launched himself at me like a rat, or a bat, from the top of the stairs. The shard dripped blood (hers and mine mingling together) and glinted among the dim triangles of light and dark.

I moved, leapt, took off towards the next set and heard Jakesie crumple into the wall behind me. He must've hit it with some force, because I heard the crunch from 15 feet away. But I didn't stop to comfort him. Oh no.

It was amazing. I mean, I could feel myself panicking, a cold fright buzzing about my senses but underneath it, somewhere, I was kind of along for the ride, enjoying this.

But now I was flying. On each landing I would land on one foot, pirouette, and spring down the next flight and let the cool air rush by my ears. I could turn, and glide, and bank to negotiate the tight angles created by the concrete mould underside of the stairs and the unrelenting drop of the walls. I am Peter Pan.

Many miles above me I heard Jakesie screech with rage – again. What a prick. I mean, what a little prick he is. I should …

Thump.

Lost it. Stopped enjoying it and I lost it. Fuck. In a heap now. And the bawling banshee is bearing down on me.

Aaargh! Fuck! My legs! My legs have gone! No juice! Fuck!

Boom, boom, boom.

Oh fuck. Jakesie's comin' tae get you.

Boom, boom, boom.

Get up. Fuck. Think.

Boom, boom, boom. Oh … wobbly. wobbly!

Legs gone. Oh no. No. Not now. Not now. Come on. Come on, Come ON! AH!

Doors – open. Through here.

The lift. Get into the lift.

Stagger through three big, heavy doors and onto a landing. God, where is he? I can't hear him here. Press the button.

30 … 28 … 26 …

Come on. Please. Please. Come on. Come on. Please. Please. Please God, I'm sorry. I'm sorry. I'm really sorry. I promise. I'll never do this again. Please. Just let it come now, please. Please. Please.

22 … 20 … 18 …

Oh, God – COME ON! OPEN UP, YOU FUCKER! OPEN UP! OPEN UP!

16.

COME ON!!!!!! OPEN THESE FUCKING DOORS!!!!! OPEN THESE…

Right. Go. Go go go go go go go go go go go go. Go …

Up. Yes. He'll never think of that.

Close doors.

16 ... 18 ... 20 ...

What if he's watching the lights?

22 ... 24 ...

Maybe I should go back down when I get to the top.

26 ... 28...

No. Then, he just needs to sit and wait on me.

...30.

No. I'll just wait on him. Where he'll never find me.

10: DEAR DAD

Dear Dad,

You should see what I can see. There's nothing, literally nothing between me and deep space.

I could fall off the world and nobody would ever know. It might happen. It might happen. That's why I wanted to write to you.

If it happens I'm ready.

I'm naked. It's nine below zero and I'm standing stark staring naked on top of this tower.

This tower I thought was so vast, is just … tiny.

I'm staring at the sheer black sky and letting the thin, certain beams of light shoot into my head. This light that left these stars a hundred million years ago, light from suns that no longer exist, light that swam through space, through swamps of time, older than the Earth, onward, onward, to come … to me. To rain down into my eyes, my skin, my head. Me. To energise and revitalise me.

I believe. I believe again.

The night's so black I can't see where the sky ends and the city begins. Stars cascade from the firmament and scatter on the black angles and dense shadows of the buildings. They scoop and swirl and show a hundred different paths, all roads to nowhere, I suppose.

But one of them's the way home. For a moment I think I can see it. Then it's gone.

If I die I know you'd be sad, but you'd also be angry. In fact you'd be more angry than sad. You'd hate me for not being careful, and hate me for being so stupid and curse me for wasting my time, my talents, my brain. For pissing away all my chances, all the ones that you never had. And I'd be a victim of drugs. I'd be your disappointment. I'd be your shame. You could never hold your head up in the Welfare Club again. But then you've always got Steven.

I'm going to die, I think. Someone's going to kill me. You don't know him and there's nothing you could do if you did and I don't want you to kill him for revenge. Please. Don't.

Of course I could die of exposure up here on the roof of these flats. Lying naked 300 feet up in the wee small hours of mid-winter probably doesn't seem like the cleverest thing to do but it's got advantages:

– If this guy comes for me I'm too weak to resist, but he might get a surprise and I'll get away.

– If he doesn't, I might just throw myself over the edge and see if I really can fly.

There is something else about it. You've never done it. You've never done what I'm doing right now. You've never seen what I'm seeing or thought what I'm thinking. You've never been me, here, now. This is something you've never done.

That's why I wanted to write to you.

I wish I had some paper.

11: BLACK STREETS

I need to get back to somewhere I recognise. This is all wrong. It's too dark here. What happened to all the stars?

Thick black clouds have swallowed up the moon and the stars and the sky and all the fallen diamonds are just puny, flickering bulbs on the end of leaning rusty poles. That's the ones that work.

And nobody's got their lights on. No parties round here. No revellers to wish me well and offer me a drink and say 'aye, come with us' as they roll on to the next party. I'm alone.

All the windows are boarded up and the dank grey pebbledash walls are covered in ugly, pointless, threatening scrawls:

lally takes it up the ars

RANGERS
RED ROXY'S MACHINES

KICK to KILL
not to thrill
POPE
E
TH
FUCK

UVF

Graffiti is just the dying clawing at walls. Very deep, son. You should be doing Philosophy.

I haven't a clue where I am. I just think I should keep checking over my shoulder to see if (Jakesie) anyone's there.

If I can get to the dual carriageway, I'll know where I am then.

There's no start or finish to these streets, they all just disappear up the arsehole of the next one. The pavements are sharp and ruptured; weeds and gravel erupt and cling to the rubbish strewn across the roads. Stagnant puddles of oil and petrol and sludge and fag ends lie like craters every few feet. There's no sense or shape to anything. It's all dank and dull and smells like it's pissed itself.

Cheap, damp settees – all torn velour and brown patterns – are discarded outside every other grey block, the latest in garden furniture. Gutted TV sets lie on their side along with bits of bikes and engines, burst black bin bags and dirty white plastic magazine racks with cloudy pictures of wilted flowers. A visiting alien could be forgiven for believing these people live a kind of hardy, alfresco lifestyle, but in fact nobody goes outdoors unless they absolutely have to. Nor will they answer the door. They're not tough. They're all scared shitless.

Squelch. Well, that's what I get for my thoughtful reverie – a soleful of dog turd. Crunchy on the outside but spreads soft and creamy on your shoes, giving it that 'impossible to get out of your tread' quality. Shit. My feet are like magnets for this stuff. Everywhere I go, no matter how careful I am, dog turds lie in wait for me. I can be carefully scanning the ground, picking my way through the dog turd obstacle course, when one wee squelchy one'll jump to the side, lurk about, then pounce under the soles of my shoes. I can almost hear them sniggering, the little basturds. My Mum used to say it's supposed to bring you good luck, but I think she just said that to make me feel better. Anyway, if it was true I'd be the luckiest guy in the world, which I'm not.

After a search I find a bit of grass long enough to wipe my shoe on. Even the grass is dead round here – all greasy and listless. Still, it cleans my shoe for now.

I decide to walk up the steep bank where this grass grows. The top of the bank is shielded by a phalanx of huge advertising hoardings, each image horrific.

A naked, emaciated wee black boy holds out a begging bowl:

IT'S CHRISTIAN AID WEEK

A sleek white car drives through a beautiful tropical scene:

THE BEST

A huge face spliced with a full length image of a tall thin man:

Barrymore – al'wight?
Sundays 7.15pm, ITV

A curvaceous, possibly naked, pale white girl looks over the shoulder of a tanned, muscular, short-haired man whose back is to the camera:

GET IT
WHILE YOU CAN,
MAN.

The paper on these was grey and weather worn except for the Barrymore one which looked like it had been newly posted and was full of livid and garish colours. Didn't he used to be on Saturdays? Oh, fuck – who cares? Stop filling your mind up with this stupid, irrelevant TRIVIA! It's shite, it's just all shite! Christ!

I wonder for a moment why these hoardings are here – to taunt people? To make them aspire to more? To make them wish they were dead? Or maybe to try and convince people that life might just be worth living. All of the above, I suppose. And a few more besides.

I look through the criss-cross supports beyond the adverts. There it was. The dual carriageway.

12: EYELESS IN GLASGOW

I am a short-sighted myopic specky peering moley gink.

I am a fucking wanker, a total prick, who is really in the shit now.

aaaaaaaAAAAAGGGGHH!

One of my contact lenses has just flicked out of my eye and now resides somewhere on this grassy verge. It was the right one.

Half blind.

Fucking great.

That's all I need.

aaaaaaaAAAAAGGGGHH!

13: DUAL CARRIAGEWAY

I got over the fence slowly and with great difficulty. It's funny how when you're wee things like that are easier. My feet and hands felt thick and clumsy and I used to be so nippy. Anyway, when I got to the top I sat astride the hoarding, kicking my shitty right heel into the forehead of Michael Bloody Barrymore. Al'wight?

The embankment on this side was far more steep and ran down towards the dual carriageway but levelled off abruptly and momentarily as it came to an end at a supporting wall. There was probably about a fifteen foot drop from there, about the same as the drop from the top of this hoarding to the peak of the embankment. I thought about climbing down at the time, I really did, but getting up had been so difficult and I thought getting down would probably be harder so I decided to dreepy down the hoarding. Mistake.

Landing with a thud, I twisted my ankle and hurt my back and slipped and slid and skidded on my back all the way down the embankment towards the dual carriageway. I thought the momentum was going to throw me down right onto the road and that'd be me, a goner. But I managed to claw my fingers into the slick earth and slow myself down, grinding to a halt on the slabs on top of the wall.

A car whizzed by below me.

I lay there facing the skies again, too sore to move. My ankle throbbed and my back ached. My ribs felt battered and bruised and the cuts on my face and hands were nipping again. That's it, I thought. I'm fucked. I've had it. No more. I give in.

Nauseous orange light lapped round my eyelids and my belly heaved, but nothing came up. Fuck. Fuck it. Just fuck it. I lay on the slab wishing it was a morgue. I'll just lie here till morning and I'll be dead and that'll be it.

So I did.

14: DEAR STEVEN

My dear brother Steven,

I am dead. This is not, however, a suicide note. No, I was murdered. So this is that thing I know you secretly have wet dreams about – one of those letters that gives a clue to the killer. Or killers. But wait, wait.

You're out in your patrol car. A message comes through ordering you back to the station. The desk sergeant leads you through to speak to the Detective Inspector. You know something is wrong. You can see it in their eyes, in their movements, in their kindness, and quietness.

'Sit down, please,' the Detective says.

You feel the nerves fluttering in your stomach. Distant echoes at the back of your mind are beginning to think unthinkable thoughts – Dad's dead. Mum's dead. Christina's dead. But you stifle the thoughts and focus on the Detective.

'Steven,' he begins. Now you know for sure it's serious. 'Steven, I'm afraid I have some bad news. Your brother's been found dead. I'm very sorry.'

Thank Christ. It's only that little twat. Still, look concerned, but stoic.

'How … how did it happen?' You will manage to stammer.

'Well, we don't really know yet. He was found lying on a wall beside a dual carriageway in one of the nasty bits of town. It's possible he died of some sort of overdose, or perhaps suicide, or possibly an accident. It … it may even be murder. We can't be sure at the moment.'

You will pause, bravely. Then: 'He must have been murdered. My brother didn't approve of drugs, and loved life too much for suicide.'

'Well … we can't rule out an accident, yet.'

(You) 'He was murdered, I tell you!'

'Constable, please … '

'I'm sorry, sir. It's just … I've got a feeling in my bones, a hunch if you like.' I always said you looked like Quasimodo.

'Yes. I understand. Believe me we will certainly do everything we can to bring his killer …'

'Or killers.'

'…or killers, to justice. You can rest assured on that, Constable.'

'But sir, can I … ?'

The Detective will raise his hand. 'No, Constable. I know what you are going to say. But you are too closely involved. I can't put you on the case.'

'But, sir! I just need 48 hours!'

'No, Constable. I'm sorry. But you know the regulations. You are, however, entitled to 48 hours compassionate leave …'

A knowing look will pass between you. You'll get up and do that special handshake you're so good at.

'We'll catch the bugger, Steven,' he'll say.

'Or buggers. Yes, sir,' you'll say.

And then they'll ask you to identify my body. Now when they open the drawer, keep your composure. Resist the temptation to pinch the nipples of my corpse. Instead, look in the front left hand pocket of my jeans. This note'll be in there, addressed to you. I'll put it there so you have to fumble about in my groin area and the boys at the morgue will think you're some latent incestuous gay necrophiliac. Which will be at least partly true, of course. Still, it'll bode well for your promotion.

The note will begin:

'My dear brother Steven,

I am dead.'

So – now you've got the note. It would be too easy to simply give you the name (or names) and address (or addresses) of the culprit (or culprits), and anyway, you want leads you can follow, clues you can puzzle over and suspects you can interrogate. Then you collar the baddy (or baddies), avenge the death of your brother and propel yourself straight into CID and the Grand Master Lodge. Neat.

Well here goes:

It was a conspiracy. The murder had, in fact, been attempted several times before.

Like the time the victim was in the attic with his brother and was inexplicably pushed down the opening to the landing and broke his leg.

Or the time in a family outing to a park when the victim's boat was inexplicably capsized into the deep, clatty water at Rouken Glen park. Luckily his brave brother and his mates were close by in another boat and they managed to rescue him, and definitely didn't push him under again three or four times before the parkie came.

Or the time when a person or persons unknown jumped him in his bed on the first morning of the school holidays and put a pillow case over his head, tied a rope around his neck, bound his hands and feet, and pulled him feet first and face down, banging the victim's chin down the stairs one by one so that he later required three stitches. Then dragging the said victim into the living-room and holding a trial where the victim was accused of being –

'A little prick.'

'A whingeing little shite.'

'A known associate of Catholics.'

'Too big for his boots.'

The victim was found guilty by his unknown persecutors and duly sentenced. And the punishment fitted the crimes.

On the first count he was sentenced to a bulldog

clip on his penis 'to make it grow'.

On the second count the sentence was to have his own faecal matter smeared round the mouth area of his still pillow-encased head.

On the third count the victim was forced to sing 'The Sash' right through twelve times and beat with a leather belt every time he made a mistake. He was also sentenced to have a red hand drawn on his torso in lipstick.

On the last count he was forced to wear wellington boots filled with ice cubes then thrown into a cold bath to 'shrink him' till the boots fitted.

Finally the victim was told to beg forgiveness for his crimes and admonished with the warning that if reports of this 'in-camera' trial ever leaked out, it would mean instant and certain death by fire.

Later that year – on Bonfire Night to be precise – the victim was reminded of this warning when a lighted cloth was thrown onto his head, singeing most of his hair. The victim was required to have his hair cut into a 'skinhead' fashion shortly afterwards.

Follow those leads, Steven. You will find the architect of the events that led to my death.

As to the other conspirators, you may wish to think about the following:

> The first is hairy, large and loud
> And yearns for his sons to make him proud
> But he's seen it, done it, bin there too
> Best place for him is in the zoo.

> The second is twitchy and lacking teeth
> She's consoled in her life by unshaking belief
> She sees good in all, even her offspring
> Which is very heart-warming, but shows
>   lack of thinking.

The third you have never met, as far as I know
He's evil and vicious and sells smack and blow
He violates that which he cannot possess
And left high in a tower, a dame in distress.

Really, Steven. She was beautiful. He cut her face open.

I should've done something. I should've stopped him. I should've killed him before he did that thing to her. She's … she'll never get over it. Every time she looks in a mirror she'll see that jagged glass. She's scarred for life. Or death.

Jesus.

I don't really hate you. I don't care what you do. You were made your way and I was made mine. There's no escaping it. I can't blame anyone for anything. Maybe you were born to be a policeman.

Water drops splash on my forehead. SPLOSH! Right in the eye. That's the other lens gone now. Great. Now I'm totally fucking blind. Great. Pitch dark, lost, knackered, scarred, and now unable to focus on anything beyond the hand two feet from my eyes. It's totally pishing down now, waterfalls of freezing cold rain pouring down over my face. Wait! Now it's official. The world has turned into a dirty watercolour by Van Gogh, that monument to blurry thinking and myopic squinters everywhere. It runs in rivulets into my eyes, rolls down my cheeks and onto the slab.

I can't lie here all night.

Maybe I'm not dead after all.

Maybe I should get up and try to get home.
I don't hate you, Steven.

But I don't love you either.

15: TEN GOOD THINGS ABOUT BEING DEAD

1. You don't have to care about anyone or anything anymore because you are dead.

2. You might get to go to your funeral in which case you can watch everybody crying and weeping and wailing and satisfy yourself how much everybody will miss you and how fondly remembered you'll be.

3. Your Dad will feel really guilty for not treating you better while you were alive.

4. Your brother (especially if he is called Steven and is a gay woofter masonic pig polisman) will also feel guilty.

5. Your ex-girlfriends will all feel guilty and miss you and will have dreams about you shagging them that night.

6. And because you are a spirit you will be able to enter into them and enjoy that experience.

7. You might get to meet God.

8. If you do, you can ask him questions like: 'The Crusades – what was all that about?' and 'Human reproduction vs. Plant reproduction – discuss.' Or 'Did you have lewd and lascivious thoughts about Beelzebub and is that why you threw him out of heaven, to put him out of temptation's way?' Or, at a pinch, 'What was the big deal about that apple?'

9. You may also get re-incarnated and you could come back as a beautiful, intelligent, rich and successful girl with great legs and great tits and you could have any sexual partner you please, male or female.

10. You wouldn't feel guilty about anything anymore. Even your Mum and Christina. Except that you might feel guilty about them feeling guilty about you being dead. And that would spoil it. A bit.

16: STUMPING

Stump, stump, stump.
Stump, stump, stump.
Stump, stump, stump.
Stumpity, stump, stump – stump, stump!

My ankle is fucking aching.
My knees are fucking aching.
My feet are fucking aching.
My hands are fucking aching.
My shoulder is fucking aching.
My cheek is fucking aching.
My head is fucking aching.
My willypenis is ficking aching.

Had to go.
Got to go home.
No money, so walk.

WALK, you wanker, WALK!
Limp, at least.

Stump, stump, stump.
Stump, stump, stump.
Stump, stump, stump.

How fucking far is it from here?
Where the fuck is here?
Where the fuck is there?
There is a wee mining village not fifteen miles from here.
Except there's no mining now.
Still.
I call it home.
For want of a better word.

It's late, so late, and the fire went out there a long time ago. But I've nowhere else to go. I'm too scared to die really. Too scared of pain. Too scared of feeling guilty. Too scared of making other people feel bad.

Stump stump stump.

Stump stump stump.

Stump stump stump stump stump. My feet are sore.

Steven's right. I am a whingeing little shite.

It must be about fifteen miles from here. Where-ever here is.

I can walk fifteen miles.

No problem.

No problemo.

No problemo at awlly all-all.

I did it in the scouts when I was …

Thirteen.

How long ago was that? Six years? Sixty years? Sixty centuries?

Just head East.

Which is this way.

I think.

Come to think of it, this probably isn't the quickest way.

Unless I get a lift.

(**Whizzzzzzzzzzzzz**)

Which I won't.

Would you?

(**W h i z z z z z z z z z z z z z z z z z z z z z z z z z z z**)

No, neither would I.

There's no hiding from the rain here.

Maybe I should get off this road and back onto the streets.

On the other side of the carriageway.

Yeh.

17: DESERT ISLAND DISCS

Doo Doo Doo Doooo, Do Do Doo Doo Dooo, Duh Duh Duh Duh Dud Dud (Da Da Da Da)Doo Doo Doo Doooo, Do Do Doo Doo Dooo, Duh Duh Duh Duh Dud Dud (Da Da Da Da ...)

Sunday lunchtimes, for me, used to begin with *Desert Island Discs*. My Mum would make herself a cup of tea, sit down with the *Sunday Post*, and listen to *Desert Island Discs* on Radio Four. My Dad, meanwhile, would read the *Sunday Mail* and decidedly not listen to *Desert Island Discs*.

When I was wee I had a mental picture of Roy Plomley, the guy that presented the show, as this handsome, sophisticated bloke in a dark blue suit – a kind of cross between Cary Grant and my Uncle Robert. His voice was so gentle, but intelligent and persistent, and he always seemed to make all these boring people I'd never heard of become interesting, even if only for a few minutes. So when I saw some old footage of him being interviewed on television once I was shocked. He was bald, with thin, erratic hair all over the place, had creaky, piggy little eyes, and looked like a skinny man who had got fat and gone to seed. He had a rather frightened look on his face, which looked as though it had melted ever so slightly from all those years in a hot studio. I didn't believe it was him when my Mum pointed him out but I closed my eyes and, sure enough, it was Mr Plo mley.

Nevertheless, the format was simple but brilliant. Each guest had to imagine he or she is castaway on a desert island, and then pick recordings of eight pieces of music to take with them to the island. On the island they had the where-with-all for basic food and shelter, but these eight pieces of music and their reasons for picking each piece – under Roy's quiet, almost subconscious probing – often laid the individual bare.

Castaways – as Mr Plomley called his guests – were also permitted to take one book with them but not the Bible or the complete works of Shakespeare as they were already there. John Cleese of *Fawlty Towers* and Monty Python rejected the Bible and the complete works of Shakespeare on the grounds he had already read them and wanted two other books as replacements. I can't remember if Mr Plomley allowed him or not, but that was one of the best ones I ever heard.

Then castaways had to select one 'luxury' object they could take with them. They already had a record player for their music, so it had to be something else, something not of any direct practical use on the island.

Finally castaways were asked if they could only take one of their eight records, which one would it be. This was a masterstroke to end on, and Mr Plomley usually pulled it off with aplomb (I wonder if that's where that word comes from?). Anyway, the best ones were always those who entered into the spirit of it and those were always the ones most floored by that question in the end. After all that paring down of what is precious to them, they are asked to part with the majority of what little they have left. Fantastic. You could hear them squirm through the radio.

Of course, nothing stays the same. Roy Plomley died and Michael Parkinson took over, then … So Lonely (so lonely) and … I'm not sure, is she still doing it? Anyway, I stopped listening to it long ago. Not cause I didn't like the new presenters – though they weren't as good as Mr Plomley – but my Mum got religion and started going to prayer meetings on Sundays and I didn't bother to get out of bed till three in the afternoon.

I thought my Mum had stopped listening to it because it was sinful or something – like she had given up smoking and drinking and buying gossipy magazines. She's a Jehovie, you know. A Witness. But no, she said she just listens to the repeats on a Friday morning now. I didn't know they did that.

Anyway I am the castaway tonight. And my first record is...

1. *Wot A Waste – Ian Dury & The Blockheads*

Wot a waste indeed. This is a song that means something when you're fucking bored out of your brains and desperate for a smoke or a drink or a pill or a screw and instead you've got to study currents in late 18th century politics. Maybe it wouldn't be so good on a desert island, though. OK. Scrap that, Roy.

1. *The Butterfly Collector – The Jam*

A poignant melody and ethereal lyric about how life can appear beautiful if you focus on one thing, but if you take a step back from that it's an almost comically pointless pursuit. That'll cheer me up of an evening staring out over the vast reaches of ocean.

This is harder than I thought.

2. *King of the Swingers – Louis Prima, Phil Harris*

The artists better known as King Louis and Baloo the Bear. This is, of course, from *Jungle Book*, the greatest film ever made. All the songs are wonderful and I love it and it makes me believe perhaps the world was a nicer place when I was wee. Did you know the four vultures are supposed to be the Beatles? And Kaa the Snake is the same voice as Winnie the Pooh?

It makes me so happy this film. Shere Khan's voice is so funny, and so menacing. I remember the first time I saw it I was shitting myself whenever he spoke. I also cried when Baloo died. Then Bagheera says this elegy for him and we realise he's still alive, but I just kept on crying. And I kept crying to the end of the film.

I saw it on video once and I still felt like crying after that bit. I suppose it was because I realised he could've died, and that he will die. Or maybe it's because he never really existed, he was just a creation of a lot of other people: Rudyard Kipling, Walt Disney, Phil Harris and lots of clever animators and script writers who nobody's ever heard of – but I loved him as much as I loved anyone who really did exist.

I suppose that's why I'm crying.

3. God Save the Queen – The Sex Pistols

Rantin', ravin' Rotten sticks it up the monarchy in Jubilee year. Brilliant stuff. But it's more than that. This song changed the world. Okay maybe not the whole world, but certainly this fucking forelock-tugging, obsequious, Uriah Heep of a country. Well, it definitely had an effect on our household, anyway.

I took a prized copy of it up to my room and played it full blast and the speakers just about blew their valves as did the family in his/her own inimitable manner.

Steven declared he would not have that crap on his stereo in his room and threatened to frisbee the record and me out of the window. I pointed out that it was our stereo and our room and challenged him to a debate as to whether material such as this which posed legitimate questions of the political and sociological status quo was more subversive than the invocations of Satan on his Led Zeppelin albums. Steven considered this for a moment then grabbed me by the balls and told me if I ever played that crap in his presence again he would castrate me without anaesthetic.

My Dad was more measured in his response. He kicked open the door of my room and ripped the plug out of the socket. He then told me he would not have that filth under his fucking roof. When I explained that the anti-monarchist, anti-capitalist sentiment of the song was very much in tune with his own, his eyes bulged and he told me to shut my Smart-Aleck mouth. 'You think you're so bloody smart, don't you? Well, you'll see, sonny boy. You'll see,' he said. Then he stomped out of the room like a Russian shot-putter failing a drugs test. But he never mentioned it again.

Our Christine just loved it. I taught her to pogo dance to it. She'd bop about the garden shouting 'God Save The Queen!' in a Johnny Rotten sneer at the top of her voice and all the neighbours would stare. It was great. It really made her happy.

Mum just ignored the whole brouhaha till it all died down. But I could tell she was not pleased at my influence on Christine. Mysteriously the record – an original on the EMI label, probably worth a few bob now – went missing shortly after she had cleaned our room that summer. Never to be seen again.

Ah, happy days, Roy. Happy days.

4. Moonlight Sonata – Ludwig Van Beethoven
I heard this at Vivienne's house once. I was waiting in the hall while she was in the toilet and I heard it echoing through from the living-room. It just seemed to speak of a different world, a world where music like that seemed to fit – light, airy rooms where there's time and space to contemplate wonderful music. Then her Mum poked her head round the door and asked me what I was doing. She made me feel like a peeping tom, disturbing her reverie like that. Her face showed such ... contempt, such disgust at my presence that it kind of spoiled the moment. But I could've liked it. If I'd had the chance.

I don't like classical music really, but the received wisdom of castaways is you have to have a long instrumental piece on your island in order to let your mind drift. So this is the only one I can think of that fits the bill, so here it is.

5. I can't think of number 5.

6. Something by a woman.
Undoubtedly I would find myself even more sexually frustrated than usual if I were on this desert island, so I'll

need something to get me in the mood for you know what, Roy. You now – nudge, nudge, wink, wink, say no more.

Wanking, Roy. Masturbating. Tossing off. Pulling the pud. Playing the one-armed bandit. Shaking the snake. Milking the bull. Spanking the monkey. Skooshing the squeezy bottle. You must have heard of it, Roy.

Come to think of it (har, har, no pun intended) I don't really like any female singers. Madonna? Oh, I know everyone goes on about how hot she is and she gets her kit off and touches herself up at every opportunity, but she's not really my thing. I've never bought any of her records and I don't think I'd really want her on my desert island.

So scrap that. We need a woman. Who do you like, Roy? Vera Lynn, eh? No, I'll pass.

I want somebody really sexy with a sexy voice. Diana Ross? Nah. Kate Bush? Mmm – maybe. Debbie Harry out of Blondie? Mmmm. But I don't really like any of their records.

Can I come back to this one?

7. The theme tune to Desert Island Discs
Doo Doo Doo Doooooooo, Do Do Doo Doo Dooo, Duh Duh Duh Duh Dud Dud (Da Da Da Da)

Doo Doo Doo Doooooooo, Do Do Doo Doo Dooo, Duh Duh Duh Duh Dud Dud (Da Da Da Da ...)

I always liked this and it's got pleasant memories for me. Also, I'd like to hear it right through to hear what it goes like, and I'd like to know who does it. Also I'd like you to do a wee introduction on the end, in your, quiet mellifluous tones.

And in case anyone thinks I'm just saying this to ingratiate myself and suck up to you, Roy, I would remind them that you are dead and there is no percentage in this for me whatsoever.

8. Sign O' The Times – Prince
The artist formerly known as ... can't put out anything

remotely decent now, but this is hot, humid, and hits you right between the eyes. It's a pity the guy capable of this now walks around with a symbol round his neck that looks as though his mammy made him wear his doorkey there in case he gets lost. Or maybe his name is doorkey. Or maybe it's meant to mean 'dorky'.

Christ. I sound like I'm writing for the music press. This isn't how it's meant to be. Why choose Prince? I don't even like Prince. Who am I trying to show off to? I suppose it's cool to include a cutting edge black artist to let the listeners know you're hip to that but ... nobody's listening. So ... with nobody listening, who do I really like? What do I really want to take as my *Desert Island Discs*?

Jesus, Roy. This is even harder than I thought. If you try to do it for real – I mean, really just try to please yourself – it's funny how all the pretensions are exposed; all the embedded opinions you thought were your own are exposed in the harsh light as somebody else's you've simply assimilated. If it comes down to it, do I really even like music enough to want to take it to my desert island? Christ, Roy! You are one crafty bastard!

5. Comfortably Numb – Pink Floyd
I don't know why this one. It just is. It's just one of those songs I've never been able to get out of my head ever since I first heard it. Which was ... I don't know. It does seem a long ago – I can picture myself in Podge's room with Panny and him listening to it. Smoking. That seems really close. But my stomach – this cold feeling in my guts tells me it was a long, long time ago.

What's it like on this desert island, Roy? Is it warm? Is there fish and fruit, and clean water to drink? Is it beautiful? Would it be beautiful to die on? To wither and starve by a glorious, radiant orange and red setting sun.

Do you lose all sense of time on it? Do you feel lonely at first, then does the loneliness pass? Can you remember things or do you forget? Does it all just corrode in the sea, washing up and down the beach till there's nothing of you or your marks or your memories left? Is that how it is? Is that life on your desert island?

(Fuck)

I'll take the works of Shakespeare and the Bible, but I probably won't read either. I've tried before, you see, and I just couldn't. No time. Could've made time, I suppose but they were … boring.

I remember at school we did *Macbeth*. 'Out, out damned spot!' He went on about that bit for hours. What's it supposed to mean? What's all that about? I asked the teacher and guess what he said? He said:

'One day you'll realise.'

Well, I still don't get it.

And the Bible? What about that? If Jesus was God, why didn't he just sort everything out back then instead of having to put us through all the shite of the last 2,000 years. And what about Muslims? And Jews? And Hindis? Are they all just going to Hell?

And what about wee babies that die before they can be saved? And what about ladybirds, and ants and vultures and wasps and flowers and potatoes and haddock and tuna and shrimps and stuff like that? Do they go to hell? What does God do to save them, or are they just here for us to eat? Maybe we should eat Hindis, or Jews, or Muslims too.

18: THE DRUG PROBLEM

The drug problem. Or should I say: The Drug Problem.

Every few months the papers run an article or sometimes a whole week of articles (called a 'campaign') where they show silhouettes of some junkies/glue sniffers/xtc freaks who are trapped by their respective addictions. The one-off article shakes its heads, wrings its hands and says 'What can be done?' – a question they don't really want the answer to. The 'campaigns' are more bullish. They are heralded a week or two in advance with the promise to 'Lift the Lid on the City's Seamy Drug Underworld' or to 'Listen to the heartbreak stories of teenage junkie's Mum'. Putrid, isn't it.

The Drug Problem. Why do these kids take it? Why oh why oh why oh why oh why oh why oh why?

I blame the parents. And the teachers. And peer pressure. And TV. And the Government. And rock stars. And unscrupulous drugs dealers (are there any other kind?). And the lack of discipline since they abolished corporal and capital punishment. Oh, yes – and the Police, especially our Steven.

Take your pick. But don't ask the question unless you've got a pre-recorded answer playing in your head, because you don't really want to hear it. Because the real answer doesn't blame anyone.

People take drugs because (whisper it) they've discovered Life Is Shite. They've found out everything they've ever aspired to is worthless, banal, pointless. They can't love, they can't hate, they can't do anything, but they can't stop thinking. Drugs help you stop thinking. Oh, not just smack or blow or acid, but prozac and whisky and tranquillisers and TV.

Anyway, that's not my drug problem. My drug problem is of a different nature at this precise moment: I haven't got any and I'm ganting for some …

thing. Any …
thing.
    A fag
        a pint
           a pill
              a tab
                 a jab
                    a joint
                       a gin
                          a sin
                            gle malt
                        it's not
                    my fault
                  it's just
                the times
            we're liv
        ing in
      today
    tomorrow
      the next day.
CHRIST! Help me! Please! Please! Give me some
    thing, any
      thing
        that can
        take a
          way this
            pain for
              no gain
                that's building up in
                  side of me
           OHPLEASE
          OHPLEASE
        OHPLEASE
      OHPLE

Cool it.

Calm down.

Be cool.

Chill.

Calm.

Calm.

A while ago my Dad and my Mum and some social worker arranged for me to see a psychiatrist. Or a psychologist. Or a psychoanalyst. Or maybe it was all three, I don't know. Anyway, I wasn't much in favour but I wasn't really bothered either and it legitimately got me off school for one afternoon a week. Thursdays it was. I don't think I said anything much for the first four or five times, but then a few things struck me.

1. I was enjoying the attention.
2. I had the hots for the doctor.

I realised this while masturbating before school one morning. I suddenly realised she was the sexiest, most desirable woman I had ever seen in my life. I couldn't get her out of my mind. Funny, I can hardly remember anything about her now. It seems like a long, long, long time ago.

Her nylons used to make a scratchy sound when she crossed and uncrossed her legs. That's what I remember. I can still get hot just thinking of that sound. But I can't remember her face, or her voice, or her office. She had nice legs, though.

Anyway, I never went back after that. In the end she was just a head shrinker trying to shrink my head to fit into some idea they have of what's normal, or …

… sane – Where the fuck am I now?

I thought I knew my way a bit better on this side of the road, but I don't recognise this at all.

I don't know this street.

I don't know this street.

I think I'd better …

'Ho!   You!'

Peering, can't see a …

'Cunt!'

Oh fuck.

Ohfuckohfuckohfuckohfuck.   Keep cool. They probably think …

'Ho!   Aye, you, ya cunt!'

Ohfuckohfuckohfuckohfuckohfuckohfuckohfuck-ohfuckohfuckohfuckohfuckohfuck.

'YOU! CUNT! C'MERE!!'   Runlikefuck.

Ohfuckohfuckohfuckohfuckohfuckohfuckohfuck-ohfuckohfuckohfuckohfuckohfuck. Ohjesusfuck. Ohfuckoh-fuckohfuckohfuckohfuckohfuckohfuckohfuckohfuckoh-fuckohfu …

'Ah say-ed: **YOU! CUNT!**

C'MERE!!'Ohfuckohfuckohfuckohfuckohfuckohfuckohf uckohfuckohfuckohfuckohfuckohfuck.Ohfuckohfuckohfuc kohfuckohfuckohfuckohfuckohfuckohfuckohfuckohfucko-hfuck. Ohfuckohfuckohfuckohfuckohfuckohfuckohfuckoh-fuckohfuckohfuckohfuckohfuck. Ohfuckohfuck-ohfuckoh-fuckohfuckohfuckohfuckohfuckohfuckohfuckohfucko-hfuck.

Intae this close. Run (fuck) run (fuck) run (fuck) run (fuck) run (fuc …) run (fu …)

ru … fu …   ru..

Fu … uh … uh … I … promise … uh … I'll … uh … quitthe … fags … uh … promise … pleas … pleas … fuh … help … pleas … God … pleas …

(Thisisafuckingtunnel. Thisisafuckingpipeline. Thisisafucking-maze. I …)

can't see a … thing …

(DarKneSS. Dark-Ness.)

Ah'm … Ah'm … (I'mfuckingblind … Ican'tfuckingsee … it'swet … soakin' … whereamah …)

OOOOOOF!

'You, ya cunt. Whit d'ye no' stoap fur whin Ah shoutit oan ye? Eh? Cunt? Cunt.'

'Please. Don't. Please.'

19: MURDER POLIS

Their voices are ringing around this fucking crumbling plaster sandstone sewer. How can somebody no' hear them? They're gonny kill me. Please … don't … Somebody. Help.

'He's greetin'. '

'Ha! He's greetin'!'

They're laughin'. Good. Help. Mum. Dad. God. Somebody. Steven. Help.

'Goat eny munny?'

'No.'

'Whit?'

'No.'

'Cunt.'

FUCK! Uh … he kicked me! He fucking ki …

OOOOooF!

Um goannie die. Theyer goannie kill me.

OOOOooF!

OOOOooF!   OOOOooF!

OOOOooF!

God. Help me. God.

OOOOooF!   OOOOooF!

OOOOooF

OOOOooF!   OOOOooF!

OOOOooF!

'Pick 'im up.   See if he's goat eny munny.'

'20 pee. That's aw.'

'Take 'is jaicket. Zit leather?'

'Aye.'

'Fine. C'moan.'

God.
Thank God.

I thought I was in trouble there for a minute.

I thought it wis Jakesie.

I've got tae move or I'm …

                                             … fucked.

Jesus. I'm broken. Like a doll. I cannae walk.

I can't walk!
I'm crippled!
I can't walk!
I …

Oh, wait. I can.
Psawwph!
Ptooooch!

I think I've lotht a tooth.

I can theel the wint thistling right through it.

Thunts. Fucking thunts. Bathtards. Fucking fucking bathtards.

I mutht've thwallowed it-th. Yeuch.

20: SWALLOWED

i'm inside the head of a giant
a great, swithering, drunken
beast of a giant
groping around its mouth
where it's
dank
and dark
and i'm blind
i
clamber
on a slimy carpet of lolling tongue, sliding
down and
down and down
on the phlegm and grog, splashing
in the puddles of spit
and snotter
till my fingers scrape against the rough walls of its teeth
and i can feel the slickness of the wall
and the scummy puddles seeping through my shoes and taste
the sickness in its throat and i can
smell the bile from its stomach and the
stench of its undigested
dinner but i'm clinging on for dear life
for dear …
… for life
and i'm too scared
too
too scared
to
lean back in
case i fall
fall

down its
gullet
its throat
and into the acids of its belly
where i'll fizzle
and writhe and die
in the bowels
of this giant
this mammoth
that doesn't even
know i'm
here

there must
be a
gap

there must be a way out
of here
there must be a
way to
breathe the
air
again
and not the fetid
rancid fumes of …

there must be a way
to call a taxi
or the cops

or my Dad
or God
or jesus
or somebody
and get out of this

what would jonah do?
what did pinnochio
do?
what did jack do?

i don't know but help me please
help me please
i don't know but
help me
please
help me

help me
help

help.

21: MIRROR, MIRROR

I'm all t-t-t-t-t-trembly and sh-sh-sh-shaky. F-f-f-f-f-fuck. J-jesus. I need a d-d-d-drink. Or something. S-s-something to s-s-s-stop the sh-sh-sh-sh-sh-sh-shaking-ing-ing-ing-ing-ing-ing.

F-f-fuck knows how they let me in. I wouldn't've. F-f-f-f-fuckers. W-wankers. They're all pished. F-fucking sozzled. She just flung the door open and said:

'Happy New Year!'

Very loudly. But she was too arsed to notice what a fucking mess I am. She was a bit of mess herself, overweight and forty kidding on she was twenty with a short black dress and a low cut front. Moreover, this bloke loomed up behind her. I thought he was going to give me short shrift, tell me to fuck off and slam the door in my face, but – no. He was even more out of it than she was. He just leeched onto her neck and rammed his hand under her neckline, starts groping her tit. While she's still talking to me. Then I think he pulled up her skirt and starts pressing himself against her backside. She forgot about me. I waltzed in. At least it was warm.

I made for here. The bathroom. It's cooler in here, but quieter too. I've just spent God knows how long on the pan, evacuating my bowels, my bladder and my stomach. All at once, at one point. I think I was bleeding out of each of them. So I lay down. And the room spun viciously. The yellow-white light was sickening and blinding (*blindness*). Now I'm here. Looking in this mirror. Staring at this face in front of me. It's a good job I'm such a moley-eyed, short-sighted gink. I don't think I could stand this in sharp focus. Also the mirror is all dirty and smeared, but I'm better as a blur. That face …
I don't even recognise it – swollen, gristled, scarred, lumpy and cut. My eyelids have blown up and drooped down over

my eyes and I can hardly see out of them. My tongue plays with loose teeth. One of them's too far gone. I twist it and pull it … **OWWW**wt. Fuck. Still. At least … Christ, I'm going to look like Joe Jordan. My jawline's stubbly

and scrawny and jowly all at once. There's a separation of skin across my cheek. Jakesie

put that there. It's a scar already. My perfect boyish features look like a battle yard. Whatever that is. Still I'm

a … live. Alive. I'll heal. I'll get better. I'll get it back. If this has taught me anything it's

Nothing. What? What was I saying? Oh yeh. Mirror. Inspecting my face. God. What a mess. What a fucking mess.

Look, it's okay. The mirror's short-sighted too. It just looks worse because it's raw. It's all blurry, it's all smeared, it's all

out of focus.

Right.

Okay.

Mirror, mirror
On the wall
Who's the fairest of them all?

Not you, for sure
That's an unfair question
But if I might
I'll make a suggestion

Go forth from here
And do not tarry
Find a girl
You'd wish to marry

Settle down
And raise some weans
Don't fuss over looks
But use yer brains

Wise words, mirror me old mate. Apart from the marrying bit and the bit about raising weans. There's no chance of me getting home the night, so: Find yourself a wee slattern and bide the night wi' her. That's the thing to do. Disne matter if she's no' pin-up material. Just a warm body wi' a bed and some flesh on the bone. That'll do nicely.

So I venture forth. I address the long queue in the hall:

'Sorry folks, but flossing's very important these days. Best to take your time and do it right. I'm sure you agree.' I grin them a gumsy grin.

Moving quickly to the kitchen – yup, there's lots of drink. And too many people too drunk to know what belongs to who. I'll have some of that. And that. And that.

Whoaaah. Lovely. Just what I need to take away the pain. I spy another mirror. Full length. A squinty peer reveals that the duds probably leave something to be desired. Shirt's manky. Trousers stained and droopy. Out of shape. Shoes …

shoes … ? What happened to my shoes? Jesus.

So no chance of pulling any supermodels tonight then.

I'm looking in the mirror, trying not to get depressed (it's temporary, you'll wash up fine) when I see this doll eyeing up my reflection. Well, I say doll. More of a cuddly toy.

She's got this maroon, crushed velvet clingy dress on and it hugs her in all the right places even if shows the bulges a bit, especially round the tum and bum. This is not a night to be choosy. She also looks pissed as a fart, standing there playing with her hair and smiling at me in the mirror. I'm in there.

'Your hair will get very tousled if you do that.'

She giggled.

'You're very tousley haired. Did anyone ever tell you that?'

More giggles.

'The Catholic Church says tousley haired girls are evil. The Pope has condemned them out of hand. He's even issued one of his Papal Bulls. It's called: 'Burn All Tousley Haired Girls At The Stake Now – It's The Only Way To Save Them. You Know It Makes Sense.' In Latin, that is – 'Ignitium Tousledumdous Femmedoms NOW!' Thankfully I'm a proddie, so you're all right.'

She giggles again.

'You're a very giggly girl too – did anyone ever tell you THAT!?'

She plants me one right on the kisser. Tongues and saliva and everything. She tastes … warm. And wet. Exactly what I'm looking for.

22: A DANCE ACROSS ROOFTOPS

You have to bend your neck right back to see the sky from here. It feels like you're at the bottom of a deep, dark hole but the strange thing is I'm walking on rooftops.

We climbed out of a window to get here. It's a vast black amphitheatre ... like standing in the pit of a grave for some Goliath, crumbling brown muddy earth sliding down the sides while you sink further into the ... or a courtyard in the middle of the towering walls of a castle, except the castle walls are just the decrepit, dissolving black sandstone backs of multi-storey tenements with little rectangles of light dotted across the faces, wan squares of yellow on the solid black. And the courtyard is composed of the rooftops of the tenement blocks beneath, awash with crisp pokes and Coke tins and plastic bottles and chip wrappers, polystyrene fast food packs, dogshite, newspapers, sweetie papers, disposable nappies, Findus frozen dinner packaging. All swirling round in the wind like restless steer before a stampede. The buildings themselves seem black and dead, like a whole city compressed and stuffed into a shoebox, clambering over itself and gagging for breath, but retching at the stench of its own decay. You can feel the dull vibrancy of countless teeming millions of desperate, barren lives all around you. And it's not there in the buildings but in the air in between – throbbing, heavy disappointment like a thunderstorm that you know is never going to break because it'll never reach the critical mass needed, just wax and wane and the dead souls wither away to be replaced by more dead souls in a neverending ...

... she giggles again, but more huskily. She pulls out a packet of cigarettes. Embassy Regal as it happens. She proffers the open pack, two ciggies sticking out, close together, one a filter tip taller than the other, both looking exposed away from the crowd. I take them both and go into my *Now Voyager* routine. You know. The one where the bloke lights both his and the dame's fags at once, then gallantly hands the dame's lit one back to her (having taken extra care not to 'cow's arse' it). Bette Davis was in it. Really. That's what he did. Apparently this was very erotic in the Thirties when the world was black and white and nobody had sex. Paul Heinrich was the name of the guy, I think. Don't ask me where I get all this shit. It's my Mum. She watches all the old Hollywood films and gives a running commentary like 'and then he got married to her, but she left him for him that was in *Ivanhoe* …' and so on ad nausem. Anyway it does the trick with the slattern. She laps it up. I decide to press on home. I give her a kiss. Rather a good one, I believe. Then I whisper:

'What's your name?'

'Fiona.'

'Mmmmmm. Fi-fi.' I nuzzle her neck and make like a vampire.

She giggles. 'You're nuts.'

'Ah! Fi-fi … l'amour, mon petite … '

She giggles again. I give it my best Charles Aznavour anglefranc Gallic charm accent while kissing my way up her bare arms.

'L'air du temps … eau de toilette… ménage à trois … Michel Plantini … Jen-er-al de Gaulle … Vichy fromagey moi … la récherche de la temps perdu … j'accuse … Jean Paul Satre … Albert Camus … Réné Descartes … Paris St Germain … mon pamplemousse …'

And she's giggling and purring and lapping this up.

'Voulez-vous couchez avec moi?'

And we do a little tango through while I hum the tune to that French song about the sea. I spin her round and bite her neck then slow, slow, quick, quick, slow across the rooftops and kicking through the midden heaps as we go. Fi-fi presses up close to me and I feel I'm making an impression on her. Yeh, Fi-fi's real impressed.

Not so impressed are one or two of the neighbours high up in this gothic, claustrophobic warren. Some call out for quiet while one in particular yells 'Shut up ya Frog bastard!' and heaves an empty beer can at me, but misses by miles. Well, yards. A few feet at least. It's hard to tell in the dark when you're gliding through the air like Astaire and Rogers. Anyway, Fi-fi l'amour sticks her hand right down my trousers and starts sucking my face off. C'est fantastique!!

When I get up for air I decide it's time for a snorter. The half bottle of vodka in the pocket of the overly large overcoat I … er … 'borrowed' from the flat comes in handy. I swig from the brown paper wrapper till Fi-fi nudges in with her nose and gets her lips around the rim of the bottleneck. She rolls her eyes at me as she does so. It's quite sexy actually. In fact, I think I'm getting a bit …

Ow! She grabs my hand and hauls me across the tarred roof, the wind blowing a parting in the tide of rubbish, like Moses going through the Red Sea. Suffer the little children to come unto me. She's still swigging from the bottle but her pants are obviously on fire. I let my head fall back and get dragged along in her slipstream, shuffling a little two-step as I go and squinting up through the looming walls at the stars still shining up there in their firmament. I notice the clouds are edging in though.

23: SHAGGING

As she bends over to pull up the sash window that leads to
(I presume) her flat, her dress rides up at the back revealing
brief white knickers below thin black tights. I fall to my
knees and run my tongue up the length of her fleshy thighs.
Suck on the tops of her thighs and onto her fat buttocks.
She presses back against my face and I'm drowning in
nylon and sweat and flesh and it tastes great. She gets a
little vibrating rhythm going as she tugs at the catch on the
window and I'm hovering over the gusset of her panties as
it emerges, swollen and bulging and aching and longing.
The window shoots up, her torso falls through, and I rip
through her tights to gnaw and chew and suck and plunge
my face into the silky wet cotton knickers (30% man-made
fibres – I can see the label) and she's wiggling and wriggling
and not giggling, but panting and puffing and pulsating.
And I'm eating away at her and I clench my teeth on the
frilly little edging and it tears and she half gasps half
screams as I pull them to the side like the clever dog I am
and stick my nose right inside then lap up the juice like the
hungry cur I am and she's moaning and loving it and
whining through her nose and shaking her ass pushing it
further into my face and then she crawls in through the
window and I'm after her, unzipping my fly and scrambling
and fumbling in the dark until I catch hold of her
staggering away from me then I'm on her and she folds
over the edge of the bed face down, arse up, offering it like
a bitch on heat and I'm tearing off the vestiges of her tights
and straining
the fabric of the knickers to get …
… to
… get

IN

there and I'm away, away, away ah-whoah-hoo!
Ah-whoah-ho-ho-ho-ho-ho-ho-ho-ho-ho-ho-ho-ho-ho-
ho-ho-ho-ho-ho-ho-ho-ho-ho-ho-ho-huh-huh-
huh-huh-huh-huh-huh-huh-
HAH!! ho-ho-ho-ho-ho-ho-ho-ho-ho-ho-huh-
huh-huh-huh-huh-huh-huh …
Huh … huh … huh … huh …

Huh-huh-huh-huh-huh-huh-huh-huh-huh-huh-
Huh … huh … huh
Ho.

Huh HAH! HAH! HAH!

Humpnnphh-ahhhhhhh-mmmmmmmm-fffffffffff

I'm …

fucked.

Hmph. Hmph. Hmph.

Oh fuck. Let me sleep.

24: MORE SHAGGING

Oh fuck. Let me sleep. No, not again. Please. Awwww-
wwww-www! Naw! Please! Oh! Fuck.. Fuckit. Fuckity fuck
fuck fuckit. Awww. Pl … mmm. Awww. Okay, okay. If you go
on top. Yeh. Mmmm. Okay. Okay. Go. Go go go go go go go
go go. Go go go. Go. Go! Go on! Go! Go! Go go go go go go
go go … g … go … go … on … go … yes … yes … Yes! Yes!
Yes! YES! YES! YES!

YES!

YES!

YES!

YES!

YES!

YES!

YES!

YES!!

OooOoOoOoOhHhHhHhHhHhHhHh ... ...

You're beautiful.

Yeh.

I love you.

Yeh.

I love you.

25: INSOMNIA

Insomnia is punctuated by cigarettes, I've found. And her snoring.

26: DEAR CHRISTINA

Dear Christina,

My first memory of you is the time you got lost. Mum was frantic, calling the police and getting all the neighbours to go out and search for you. I was only about four at the time and was left in the house with Steven, who told me it was all my fault.

I remember Dad came in from work and grabbed Steven, screaming in his face, demanding to know what had happened. Steven told him I had told you Mum would give you into trouble for wetting your pants, which might have been true. I can't remember. I just remember walking into the kitchen and you were sitting on the floor in the middle of a wee green puddle, playing with your dolly. Then you burst out crying and I got upset and started crying and went out to get Mum who was in the back green hanging out washing and talking to Mrs McAllister next door. By the time I got her attention and brought her back into the kitchen, the little green puddle was still there but you were gone.

Dad glared at me then tore out the door to join the search party. Steven kept saying you were going to die, you were going to get run over by a lorry, or a stranger would come and take you away and we'd never see you again. Whatever happened would be my fault and I would have to live with the fact I was responsible for my sister's death. I would get taken away and spend the rest of my life in a home and nobody would ever want to speak to me again. Then a policeman came in and asked me what happened and I burst out crying again.

Those were the longest hours of my life. I remember sitting in the living-room with Steven and the policeman and nobody saying a word. The clock just kept

ticking, ticking, ticking. The big eye-shaped clock that
stood in the centre of the mantelpiece – remember? No, of
course you don't. I'll never forget it. I couldn't even tell the
time but I can still hear the ticking in the middle of my
brain right now. It started to get dark but nobody switched
the lights on. We just sat there – PC Plod, Steven, and me.
The polisman went to the toilet at one stage and Steven
started again – Dad's going to thrash you, Mum'll never
forgive you, Christina's being eaten alive by bad men and
it's all your fault. I didn't cry this time. I just sat there,
agreeing with every word.

   Steven fell asleep. I remember I felt really tired but
promised myself I would not go to sleep until they came
back with you, safe and sound. And if they didn't, I
resolved, I would never sleep again. I feel a bit like that
again now.

   I've done a bad thing you see, Christina. I'm here
with this woman, in this bed, and she thinks I love her and
I don't. I told her I did, but I don't. That's why I can't sleep.
Maybe.

   Whenever I've done a bad thing I think of you.
You are my confidante, my confessor. In you I can trust,
utterly and completely, because I know you'll never breathe
a word of it to anyone. Ever.

   I don't know what time it was when they found
you that day, but it was late. Later than I'd ever been
allowed up. You probably don't even remember any of this.

   They found you fast asleep in Mr Melrose's pigeon
shed at the end of the street. Or rather, Mr Melrose did.
Safe and well and covered in pigeon shit and straw. You'd
just wanted to pet the birds. If Mum hadn't panicked and
sent out everyone to search the highways and byways, Mr
Melrose would've fed his pigeons at the normal time and
found you then.

   If.

   You won't remember. But I can't forget. Especially

I can't forget what happened after the policemen left. Dad turned round and looked at the three of us – his children, his progeny – and did something I never ever remember him doing before or since. He fell to his knees and threw his arms around us and hugged us to within an inch of our lives. Unbelievable. Although I was only wee, I know he could never have done that before because I can remember – I can feel it keenly, even now, just thinking about it – how totally and utterly *shocked* I was. I think he might even have been crying, or at least on the verge of tears, because I remember his shoulders going up and down, I remember the vibrations that seemed to be coming from him and going through all of us. Then, he did that thing. He did that thing that Dad always did so well.

He thrashed me. Steven was right after all. There we were, everyone all relieved, smiling and crying and hugging and happy families and then … he just couldn't take it. He started wagging his finger and telling me how I had caused a panic and that I was a bad boy for being a wee clype and then … he just took me over his knee and smacked my bum hard. Five times. I remember. I couldn't believe it. I still can't I suppose.

I never blamed you, though. I never held it against you. I loved you. Even though it was really hard having you as my sister. My big wee sister, my wee big sister. When I was at school everyone used to taunt me about my 'mongol sister' or my 'spastic sister'. I used to go mad, because you weren't either of those things. You had a mental age of three and that was never going to get any better, but you weren't a mongol or a spastic. So even at four, I was supposed to be responsible for you, even though you were four years older than me.

Of course, you did get a bit better. Now they reckon your mental age is six or even seven. But I've still overtaken you, years ago. It's really strange, you know, getting older than someone born before you. That's what it was like. I remember playing with you and everything being fine and good fun, and then you would throw a tantrum and I'd get the blame. By the time I was seven or eight, you were boring. When I got to nine or ten, you were a drag, an embarrassment. Something I had to lug around, keep an eye on, be aware of, make allowances for. But I never hated you. I always loved you. Because I knew you loved me. Pure, unconditional love. Given freely. And that's why when I've done something wrong or unworthy, I've always come to you. Because I know you'll forgive me.

 'S'alright, boy,' you say.

 And you never told anyone. Because you never remembered anything, but I knew I could trust you. But I know you remember that day we were out on the back green, just wrestling and clowning about. It was hot and sunny, and we'd been having a water fight, skooshing Fairy Liquid bottles at each other and rolling about on the grass, amongst the daisies and buttercups. Dad came out and told me to cut the grass and I shuffled off to the shed to get the lawnmower. When I came back you were crying. Dad said you were going to go away to a special school and we'd only see you at holidays and some weekends.

 He never quite understood you, Christina. No, that's not quite right. He didn't want to understand you, because that would've meant his accepting you and that was one thing he could never do. It would've fucked up his little world view he got from reading Party leaflets on Darwin and Marx: Evolution and the historical inevitability of the triumph of Socialism. You see, he believed he was part of an unbreakable chain of progress, leading to the emancipation of the human race from the tyrannical yoke of capitalism, sickness, poverty and ignorance. We were the next links in his chain, the vehicles by which his genes would eventually bask in the sunny light of socialist equality and freedom for all.

 Funny things genes. One little flicker so minuscule,

so microscopic, and your whole life's changed. Your whole family's life's changed. The whole world's changed.

Steven, being the eldest, got all the encouragement and attention as he was the best bet for re-creating Dad. Or so Dad thought. But, despite his left-wing philosophies, he wanted a 'gentleman's family' so he was over the moon when his little girl was born. Except, of course, you were written off as a bad investment and barely got so much as a glance in your direction after that. It took him a while to get over you, but then I came along to complete the picture. Another boy, but a hedge against Steven being run over or something. But the bastard never bothered his shirt with me either. Always a union meeting or a party conference or something to go to. Until I was sixteen. When I passed all my exams with flying colours. Suddenly I was the first in our family – the first in all the generations stretching back to the primordial soup of randy amoebas – who could get a university education. A clear step forward. Now I was the bee's knees, the cat's whiskers. A chip off the old block. Steven was an also ran.

I wonder now whether he twigged about then that Steven was gay. I'm still not sure. I think he knows, but just doesn't want to admit it to himself. I can't imagine Steven telling him. Especially now as they won't speak since our lad joined that instrument of establishment oppression and control, Strathclyde Police Force.

So I became the best chance the family has of 'continuing the line'. With a university degree, too, if he has his way. Biggest fucking mistake he ever made. I may now be his only real hope as a receptacle for his gene pool, but it's at a price. I'm smarter than him. And he knows it. He hates us all now. Mum for her Conversion and Christianity, Steven for his Queerness and Policedness, Me for my Smart-assedness and Drunkeness, and you, love, for your Retardedness and Ungainly Gait. All of us, equally, for our betrayal of him.

I remember once I'd been caught shoplifting at Boots the Chemist in town. Somehow I'd managed to convince the polis to let me tell my parents before they did. He was away at some T.U.C. school in England but would be back the next day. I just kept hoping against hope that if I didn't say anything the whole thing would be forgotten about. And nothing happened. There was no knock at the door from Inspector Plod on the night he got back or the night after that. I began to think I'd got away with it. After all, it was only two bottles of Old Spice aftershave. I was probably doing them a favour in a roundabout way. Then, three days afterwards, it just got too much. Not the theft, but the fear of them – him – finding out. So I told you. You, lying in your bed, sleeping the sleep of the innocent. And that's when I saw you, for the first time, as what you might have been.

The moonlight bathed your features. Your face, usually contorted or twitchy, was for once composed and peaceful. Your eyes, always flickering around for a focus or staring vacantly, were closed and still. And I saw then that you could have been beautiful. A beautiful young woman with promise and plans and potential rather than the eternal infant frozen in a discoordinated, distorted, ten sizes too large body. You were beautiful. You are beautiful. Probably the most beautiful thing I have ever seen in this world. My burden, my solace, my confessor. My big wee sister.

I wish I could write this down and send it to you. I wish you could receive it and know how to read it.

I wish … I wish …

27: NOW I LAY ME DOWN

Now I lay me down to sleep
I pray the Lord my soul to keep
If I should die before I wake
I pray the Lord my soul to take

and prayers …

and letters …

and..

28: VIRTUAL TELEVISION

'Hi. Welcome to the show.'

Oprah's in the middle of the studio audience with her serious face on, speaking to the camera. 'Today we examine the talking tattoo people.'

I'm slowly startled as I realise I'm a guest. I try to peel myself from the sticky leatherette swivel chair. I'm sitting on a raised dais with six other sorry cases, all naked and all in various states of tattoo. Oprah heads for the old guy on the extreme left, her impossible stilettos screeching like the tines of a fork on a window pane.

This guy's pushing seventy and he's got a huge, blue picture of Margaret Thatcher peeking through the grey undergrowth on his chest and abdomen. Oprah leans on her hip and pouts.

'Alex. Hi. This is Alex from Wisconsin, everybody, and he has ...'

'A picture of our beloved Margaret ...' he pipes up in a Polish accent.

'... a picture of the beloved Margaret Thatcher on his chest. Yes? Right. So how long've you and Maggie been together, Al?'

Oprah smirked unworthily as the guy blubbered on incomprehensibly. She looked just the same as she does on telly, except bigger. Her skin was a beautiful milky coffee colour and her eyes dark brown jewels in pools of pearl white and she looked good now she finally had her figure under control.

I suddenly remembered I was naked, and panicked at the thought of becoming aroused on network television. I try to take my mind off it and look along the line to my right. I'm dazzled by the hot, unrelenting brightness of a studio light staring straight at me, and draw my seat back. In the next moment, the light is eclipsed by the shape of an attractive young woman with soft pink petal skin, absently running her finger along the swell of her breast. She smiles at me. I smile back. She smiles again, swings her seat through ninety degrees and crosses, then uncrosses her legs. Little beads of sweat prick through my forehead. I know her, I know her name – I just can't think of it now. She looks back over her shoulder and raises a wicked eyebrow. The orange head of a lynx on her shoulder blade suddenly snarls and moves to leap out at me. I swing back to the safety of Oprah and the old Pole.

Oprah is giving the guy a kind of mock respect. 'Can I speak to your tattoo? Do you mind?' The guy shakes his head in affirmation. Oprah flicks a conspiratorial look at the camera and asks: 'Lady Thatcher, how does life on Mr. Dziekinowski's torso compare with running the English Parliament?'

The Maggie tattoo launches into a tirade that begins 'Johnny Major is a back-stabbin' little toid ...' but the phoney Brooklyn accent strips her of any credibility.

I squint beyond the lights at the studio audience and notice my Dad and Mum sitting together in the third row from the back. My father looks just the same as he always did, except a little heavier, a little greyer and now sporting a moustache. He sits in a sensible V-neck, arms folded, enthralled by Oprah. My Mum, like the most of the rest of the audience, is raving, screaming that the end of the world is nigh and begging for forgiveness and delivery from evil. She barks at Oprah to sanctify her soul in Jehovah's love but Oprah's a pro and presses on regardless.

Oprah's now on the next one, a middle-aged woman sitting next to me, in fact. Oprah's body seems to have inflated slightly. As I watch, her body's getting bigger and bigger, blowing up so she looks like the Michelin Man or the Goodyear Blimp or something, but her head remains the same size and she seems oblivious to her embarrassing condition. I can't say exactly when but her body slowly stopped growing, but her head started to get smaller and her voice was like an erratic tape recording, going fast and slow and high and low and slurred and Pinky and Perky-like.

I'm horrified but still super-glued to my seat. I know I'm terrified but haven't admitted what the fear is yet. It's my tattoo, it must be. What will my tattoo say? What dark secrets will it reveal about me? I'm too scared to look to find out where it is or what it's of.

My erotic neighbour nudges me. I can't look at her (Viola ... ?), but hear her whisper –

'Look, Santa Claus is operating camera four.'

There is indeed a man in a red suit and sporting a bushy, whitish beard behind the apparatus but I can see – even with his earphones as a disguise – that it's not Santy, but Karl Marx. Dad catches my eye and he smiles and gives me the thumbs up. I decide not to disillusion the temptress (Vi ... Viv ... acious ... ?) for fear I may have to put an arm round her and get it bitten off by that bloody lynx.

(Vivienne?)

Oprah's now towering over me, pinning me to my seat with vulturous, vicious eyes. No longer the well-paid TV personality, she's a seven foot emaciated harridan, a brown leather skeleton teetering on heels and hanging over me like a bowed branch ready to whiplash.

'Why are you here! Why are you wasting my time! Why don't you answer me!' she harangues.

But it's too late. My legs have already turned into tree trunks and my toes to roots scrabbling through the floor. My arms and fingers quickly follow suit and, as my stomach and chest go under ... the small, blue tattoo on my neck flaps its wings and flies away.

29: BIRTHS, DEATHS & MARRIAGES

'Vivienne! Who the hell is Vivienne!'

Fi-fi's going ga-ga and I don't know what the fuck is going on.

'You BASTARD! You BASS-TARD! How could you do this to me!!'

She's tearing and screaming at my face, sweating and convulsing and writhing on the bed. I jump up – it's wet. God! I've peed it! I've … no, wait. Not me. My pants are dry, apart from a wet patch on the bum. No leaky willy here, thank you. It's her. The mattress is like Loch Lomond and she's screaming at me and … what've I done? What the hell is happening here?

I fumble around in the dark, bump my head on something and career through newspapers and empty bottles and crap all over the floor. It's like all that garbage from the rooftops has blown in through the window. I hit a wall and grapple along it till I find a light switch. The 100-watt blares on with the frilly weave of the tatty shade throwing shadows across the room. It's like a war zone. Rubbish everywhere. Peeling wallpaper, dirty clothes, unwashed dishes – just crap everywhere. Fi-fi's house-keeping standards are not quite up to my Mum's.

'What the fuck is up with you?!' I inquire politely.

A torrent of abuse comes back, sounding more like a drain gurgling its last gulp of water than identifiable words or phrases, but I can see she really is in some distress. There's something wrong.

'What's the matter with you? What's wrong? Are you sick or something?' I'm keeping my voice fairly calm, fighting this rising tide of panic in my chest. This is serious. She lets go another scream that resounds through the pores of my skull and out through the walls of the building, causing the foundations to tremble. Oh fuck. She's dying or something. This is serious. Think. Do something. Get help.

'I'll get help.'

'No-oo-oo-oo-ooh! Don't **go!** <u>**Stay with me!**</u> **Pleeeeaaase!** *I'm frightened!'*

You're frightened! You're scaring the shit out of me, lady.

'No, it's alright, it's alright. I'll just be two minutes. Honest. Where's the phone?'

No direct reply to that one. Instead she draws her knees up to her chest and shakes and strains and quivers like she's constipated. I bolt to the hall.

It's darker in here. No windows, and no light bulb in the fitting. Move away from the bedroom door and there's no light at all. Suddenly a door further along opens and a shaft of light breaks in. A tiny wee girl pads through. She's still sleepy, rubbing her eyes and clutching a lurid purple teddy of some sort. Her nightgown is a manky 'Thundercats' T-shirt meant for a ten-year old. She's about two, maybe three years old if she's lucky. Her hair is mousy brown and so's her face, like she's been eating chocolate in her sleep.

'Mummy?'

She's a wee bit scared. I'd better watch. 'No, darling. Your mummy's fine. Is there a phone?'

'Daddy? I ... me?' She says sleepily.

Fee-fi-foe lets rip a belter of a screech and the wee one freezes, face a mask of fear and horror.

'It's okay, it's okay. Mummy's just feeling a wee bit yucky. I want to get a doctor.' I take a step forward. She's trembling.

'Don't hurt me ...' she says.

Now it's my turn to freeze. I feel sick. Something's sluicing round my head. Something's not right here. Something ...

'Please don't hurt, mummy.'

I step backwards into the bedroom, falling over a toddler tricycle as I do. On the bed, Fee-fi's squatting and mewling, her face red, her veins bulging. She opens her eyes for a moment and looks in my direction then closes them again. She's emits a low whine that becomes a dry howl that turns into a chilling death rattle. Jesus. This is scary. This is fucking frightening.

She's having a baby.

She's having a fucking kid. What the fuck have I got into here? I … I …

'*Help me …*'

I fucked a pregnant woman. I … must have. She must have been … I mean …

'*Help me-ee …*'

She's having it. She's having it now. I go to the bed. Her eyes are pleading, begging, beseeching.

'*Do something.*'

I don't know what to do. I hold her hand.

'*Please. Help me.*'

She's crying now. The tears course through little valleys in her make-up, eroding them into wrinkles as they go. I'm holding her hand and she's gripping it tighter and tighter, but she feels a million miles away. I feel like a space probe orbiting a strange planet, observing volcanoes and continental shelves crashing below.

'*Please.*'

I'm talking back to her but I don't know what I'm saying. It doesn't matter really. She's on her own now and she knows it. She's crushing my hand, squeezing the bones to pulp, but I can't feel it. I can't feel a thing. All I can do is watch.

She throws her head back on the pillow and her pelvis into the air. Her lower body is naked, exposed, vulnerable. I can see her abdomen moving. The lips of her vagina are red and sore, but they don't look like lips any more – more like the hard red rim of a wine glass. She lets go of my hand and grips the underside of her thighs, bearing down, down, down, down, down, down, down, with a motion like sit-ups but …

Oh God.

I can see the crown of the head.

'I can see the head.'

She heaves a sigh of relief for a split second and suddenly her face is beautiful. Our eyes meet for a moment. I'm with her again. I can help her here.

'It's coming through … it's … through! I can see it … it's … it's … '

It's weird. It's strange. It looks like an alien.

She heaves again – great, final push summoning all her strength, all her being, all the power of the universe into the birth of this child.

'AAAAAAAAAAAaaaaaaaaa aaaaaaaaaaaaaaaaaaaaaaaaaaaa aaaaauuuuuuuuuuuuuuuuuuuu- uuuuuuuuuuuuuuuuuuuuuuuuuuu- uugggggggggggghhhhhhhh- hhhhh!!!!!!!!!!'

It's there. Lying on a puddle on the bed. The cord is pulsing, beating.

But it has a cowl over its face.

It's dead.

A still-born. A never-alive.

And she's weeping.

'What is it? What is it? Is it a girl or a boy?'

'It's a boy.'

'A boy! A boy!'

'It's dead.'

I know. I know. Too brutal. But what else can you say? It's dead. Deader than me. But only just.

She picks it up, oblivious. It's like I never said it.

She's cooing and preening this thing, this no-thing, this corpse. She peels back the gossamer chrysalis from its face and unwinds the umbilical cord from around its neck. She's very gentle, very loving. Tender is the love. She's smiling, kissing its forehead, stroking its hair, loving it. After a moment she pulls aside the cup of her brassiere and eases her breast from it. She offers it a nipple. Its mouth falls open. She laughs, besotted with it, marvelling at it, not seeing what I see. Not seeing it like I see it.

I can't take any more. I head for the door.

In the hall the toddler is lying asleep, cuddling into her purple teddy-thing. I pick her up gently and carry her back to her room. It's in the kitchenette. The room stinks. The cat's litter tray is overflowing. Empty tins and crusty plates are everywhere. Her cot is by an electric fire with two bars on full, making the place uncomfortably hot. I place her in her cot, trying not to disturb her.

'Daddy?' she says, but doesn't wake.

I turn one bar of the fire down and switch off the light, closing the door behind me.

30: THE ABATTOIR

Snotters and bogies are just house dust, and house dust is just dead skin. Dead human. Part of you that is gone on. No need to be ashamed. No need to hide. It contains your DNA, your energy to give life. Energy is never disposed of, only changed into another form. That kid exists elsewhere. Its bits, its energies do anyway. The biological imperative is bunk. I don't need to reproduce. I am just a temporary collection of energy bound to dissipate and transmute at some future date. In fact it is happening constantly.

Walking through this ancient city in this dead of night, if you're quiet … if you're very

very quiet … it's just possible to feel the skin and bones of all the people and trees and plants and horses and animals and things that have tramped this line before you.

Ley lines. Tracing out the paths of the city like veins beneath the skin.

I am walking over the skin of the city.

I'm at the doors of the abattoir. This is where they know about killing. In the silence, you can hear the phantom calls of the dead animals.

I remember coming past here on the bus one morning.

There was a commotion and a big traffic jam piling up. I was getting nervous because I thought it was going to make me late for a lecture (this was early on, the first couple of months when I still cared about such things). I heard the driver explaining to someone a cow had escaped and was stampeding off down the main road in a bid for freedom. Some people laughed. A girl behind me said 'Poor thing. I hope it gets away.' I was raging, clenched teeth. Just k-k-k-k-kill the f-cking thin – I said. The girl looked at me. I didn't turn round. It doesn't matter, I reasoned. It's going to die anyway. So are we all, she said, looking at me strangely. Just kill it an stop it messing up our lifes, I said. Good idea, she said. Why don't you start and show us all an example.

Then the beast hoves into view. The bus seemed to lurch as the whole top deck breenged over to gawk. This big Friesian gallops down the pavement, scattering startled proles in its path. Two guys in blood covered overalls are haring down the street in its wake. It's like a parody of one of those 'bull run' things they do in Spain or Mexico or wherever. People are laughing. People are shouting. But the beast is running for its life. Its eyes are full of fear. It probably smelt it when it was packed into one of those lorries with the wooden slats, like Jews in a freight train, World War II. The stench must've been overpowering by the time it got here. The rotten, ingrained stench of death, imbued in every brick of this … this slaughterhouse. Abattoir. What a nice French sort of word.

And this animal – this beast, is running down the street. As it passes me its eyes lock onto mine for a fleet second – help, it says. Help. The girl is right. I am right. Its heart must be thudding, pounding, bursting in its great breast, ready to explode when … it does. The thing just falls over, pole-axed, banjo'ed. Except nobody touched it. It just dropped down dead. Heart attack. Heart attack. Heart attack.

Heart attack.

(cough)   *cough*

(A splutter)   *splutter!*

Head thumping.

Lungs and windpipe feel

raw, dry like the backdraft of a housefire just blown through them.

I'm gasping.

I'm dying.

I'm …

How did I get here?

I ran.

No, I mean: How did I get here? (That was not your wonderful wife, that was not your wonderful kid, that was not your wonderful life …)

You ran.

Yes, right.

Breathe.

Breathe. Breathe, you fucker, brea …

You're okay.

You're alright.

You are not a bad person.

They were nothing to do with you (you).

They were not your responsibility. (Oh no?)

We are each responsible for ourselves only. (Steven)

They were lumpen proles. (Dad)

They would only have brought you down. Held you back. (Mum)

Stopped you reaching your potential.

You owe them nothing. (no-thing)

Forget it. Just forget it. Forget them. Fuck them. All of them. Fuck them, fuck them fuck them fuck them fuck them fuckthemfuckthemfuckthemfuckthemuckthem

then run away.

Stop this in my head.

Someone.

Mum, Dad, God, someone.

Please stop this.

31: DEAR MUM

Dear Mum,

What's happened to me? What have I become? I don't even know who I am any more. I don't even know who I am.

I used to be the centre of your world. You used to be the centre of my world. We're not even on the same planet any more.

I blame Jehovah. And whatever he did that required so many Witnesses.

There's no protection, Mum. Nothing. Anything can happen to you. To me. To the world. At any time. Jehovah is not watching. He doesn't even care. He isn't there. He's nowhere. He's a construct, a concept, a convenience. A con, for short.

You … I … you carried me in your body. For the first time – the first time – I'm beginning to appreciate what that meant. I am part of you. You are part of me. You see? I am part of you, you are part of me. That's real.

I was a difficult birth, I know. You told me enough times. A double breach. Finally a Caesarian section – almost too late. And I was the baby – spoiled, Dad said. Spoiled by you. Your favourite. While Steven was always trying to live up to Dad, and Christina always a burden, I was yours. And you were mine. My Mum. My Mother.

You used to talk to me, for hours on end when I was wee. Steven would be at school, and Christina playing with her dolls, but I would sit on the kitchen floor and you would talk away to me. You told me how you and Dad met, at a dance in town. You were a Catholic and while he walked you home you asked what school he went to. And he said: 'If you're trying to inquire after my religious convictions, I'll tell you I have none. I am a Communist and an atheist.'

You were shocked, and your family disliked him, but you went on seeing him. Your mother disowned you when you married in a registry office. I never got to meet Grannie Rooney.

You used to cuddle me and tell me stories and do all the things Steven wouldn't let you do with him, and you couldn't with Christina. I loved you so much. I used to think you were so beautiful. And I suppose Dad was quite handsome when he was young, at least you obviously thought so, and the photos seem to bear you out, partially. But you were something else – a princess, a goddess, a queen. I remember just watching you when I was – oh, I don't know, three, maybe – and you were singing away to yourself, getting dressed in front of the mirror to go out. I'll never forget that.

And I think of you now. A shambles. A shivering, nervous wreck. Old before your time. Eaten up by guilt – about Christina, about rejecting your religion, about Steven's homosexuality, about the fact that you don't love Dad any more.

You changed, Mum. You changed. But I don't know why.

I realised I was changing. Growing up past Christina. Getting big enough to make Steven think twice about battering me. Getting smart and brave enough to answer Dad back. But that was all to be expected. Part of growing up. Seeing your parents and siblings as people, same as everyone else instead of paragons, or demons, or fools. But you *changed*. I didn't expect that. What happened? What happened to you?

This change … not on the outside. Well, not at first. That came more gradually, in an onslaught of nervous tics and obsessive behaviour, endlessly cleaning the cooker. But at first it was like … like … *Invasion of the Body Snatchers*. You know that film where an American small town is slowly taken over by creatures from outer space who gestate in great green pods until they are ripe. Then they burst forth, looking exactly the same as individual local townsfolk, doppelgangers, but the original person disappears and is replaced in their sleep. They look exactly the same, sound exactly the same, but … aren't. They all think the same and believe the same things. Time was you could've told me who starred in it, who directed it, who they were married to, who they got divorced from and what year they got nominated for an Oscar. But not now. All that mindless trivia banished from your mind to be replaced by … well more mindless trivia, except it's chapter and verse from the New World translation of the Bible.

They used to scare me, your Witness friends. All smiley and helpful. All shiny and scrubbed. Rose and Joyce and Iain and Belinda and George and Joseph and all those others who started coming round to the house. They were so pleasant, but if Dad or Steven or me walked into the room when you were having one of your 'discussions', it all went very quiet, apart from the loud smiles. I remember Dad and you arguing into the night. He was outraged – affronted at the thought of his wife, his woman, falling for all that 'oppressive, hocus-pocus claptrap'. I enjoyed that at first, of course. I enjoyed seeing him apoplectic all the time, seething with anger, but unable to do anything about it. How did he explain that down the Welfare Club, I wonder?

Perhaps he said: 'My wife and her cronies claim Jehovah and Jesus are the answer to everything – famine, disease, poverty, inequality, pollution, ignorance, hate, war. Meanwhile we here at the Welfare Club contend the same thing, except that we would substitute Marx and Engels for the two J's. In truth both sets are the same thing – absolutists. There are no absolutes. Nothing is wholly black, or white, or good, or evil, or right, or wrong. Nothing. And we're just going to have to learn to live with that.'

Somehow I doubt it.

D'you remember the time he actually tried to

involve me in it? To buttress his argument in the ongoing debate that stretched out over … oh, I don't know – months, years, maybe – he said, unexpectedly: 'Tell her – you're an educated lad – tell her it's a load of mythical codswollop, invented by ruling elites to keep the masses in line.'

'Actually,' I said in reply, 'any philosophy which has endured and, indeed, thrived, over a period of two thousand years – or more if you include its antecedents in Judaism – must have some fundamental truths at its core. I would have thought.' I think that was the first and last time he ever asked for my back up in an argument.

But Mum – oh, Mum. You got weird. First there was all that stuff about your blood. No transfusions. No transplants. Blood is sacred. Then we couldn't watch *Larry Grayson's Generation Game* because 'Homosexuals Are Evil'. Then it was trying to get rid of the television altogether, until creepy George managed to convince you that it wasn't the conduit for the brain-rotting pus of Satan – which shows how much he knows. But he did encourage you to get Steven and I to purge our record collections, particularly Steven's heavy metal catalogue, which I supported whole-heartedly.

Then it was us cringing when you went on the door-to-door 'missions', punting *The Watchtower* and *Awake*. All the neighbours too embarrassed to look you straight in the eye – some downright hostile. Especially after you decided to go on the mission on Christmas Day. Now that was folly. I had supported you – kind of – but if I'm being honest it was as much to wind up Steven and Dad as any kind of empathy with your beliefs. But I defended your *right* to those beliefs in the best British democratic tradition. But going out on Christmas Day to chap people's doors and ask them to give up Christmas while they're opening their presents and eating their turkey and watching Morecambe & Wise was just downright nuts.

Or maybe not. Maybe you were being subtle, knowing that if most people's houses were like ours, then people were enduring Christmas rather than celebrating it. But a wild-eyed zealot interrupting their pagan rites probably wasn't the best tactic. Even creepy George admitted that in the end.

By the way, it was dead obvious you fancied creepy George. Everyone could see it. Steven asked me if I had noticed it. In fact, I noticed Dad first – he was turning greener by the day. And it was so chaste and restrained, so frustrating and plainly an exquisite torture through which you could privately demonstrate your piety to Jehovah. Ah, sweet.

So we don't celebrate birthdays, or Christmas. Or New Year. It's a wonder we know what year it is at all. But it was fine by me. The thing I couldn't stand in the end … despite my stance of defending your right to freely state your beliefs … was that overweening, unrelenting, insufferable *smugness*. YOU were going to be saved. YOU would be redeemed to walk forever in Jehovah's Kingdom on Earth, while WE, the sinners, the unrepentant, were doomed to walk the netherworld gnashing our teeth with 99.99% of the rest of humanity since time began. But YOU, the Jehovies, George and Joyce and Beth and all the rest of them, would whoop it up in Paradise for evermore. And there would be no disease, no crime, no poverty, no death. No memory of loved ones who didn't make it. No cloud in the everlasting blue skies which would ever prick that part of your consciousness to remind you of me, or Dad, or Steven. Of course Christina would be there with you. She was innocent. Then I said – but she swears, she takes the Lord's name in vain. I even taught her to exclaim 'For Jehovie's Sake!' just to worry you.

So you started taking her to the meetings in the Kingdom Hall. And she got into it. In fact, she loved it. All the wee kids used to play with her – that's why she loved it, not because Jesus had entered her soul. And she began to believe she was going to Paradise.

I found her skipping round the garden one day, singing: 'I'm going to Paradise, Jesus is my saviour!' And she saw me and ran up to give me a hug. 'Are you going to Paradise, boy?'

'I'm not allowed, sweetheart.'

'Well, if you're not going, I'm not either.'

I never loved her more than at that moment. She wept buckets, but she stopped going to that place with you. For a while at least. Until you pressured me into going too, just so Christina would come back.

If I thought they were creepy in the house, they were even worse in there. All joyously anticipating the end of the world. It was going to rain nuclear missiles, but it's OK! We'll be fine! The Lord God Jehovah will protect us! And all that phoney questioning – raising their hands to ask the leader flaccid questions which just re-enforced beliefs rather than actually testing them. So I put my hand up.

'Why did Jehovah do it?' I asked.

'What?'

'Why did He do it? I mean, what has been the point of subjecting everyone who has ever been born to all that misery and anguish? Because Eve ate an apple? Don't you think his punishment for that has been just a wee bit over the top?'

No reply. The guy on the platform's puce with rage. Creepy George is hissing something in the pew behind me.

'I just don't get it, you see,' I continue. 'Why? What good has all this suffering done? Has it satisfied Him? Has He got some kind of twisted pleasure from all this?'

'The evils of the world are Satan's doing!' somebody pipes up.

'Yeah, but if Jehovah's all powerful, why didn't he just overturn Satan's doings and re-establish Eden? Why didn't he just punish Satan instead of us? I mean, I know he cast the little cherub down for his pride and all that, but if Jehovah's so great, why has he tolerated all this crap from Beelzebub for the last several millennia? Oh yeah – free will. So we have the choice between good and evil. Yeah, right. Of course, there is no choice in the end, because every infinitesimal thought, movement, decision is pre-ordained. We are pre-programmed by Jehovah to perform exactly the function and role He wishes. Stands to reason, doesn't it. I mean – take Judas? Supposing he'd said: "Well, Jesus isn't such a bad bloke after all and I'm quite flush this month anyway, so I don't need any extra money, so I'll just keep schtumm." The whole story would've got messed up then, wouldn't it. The whole eternal plan knocked out of kilter. So he didn't have a choice, did he? None of us do. Certainly not in the end, because if we don't choose His way then we all get exterminated come the final reckoning. Very fair. So why not be open about it and eliminate the choice factor right at the start? Why should we have to put up with our brutal lives because Jehovah can't get his finger out and sort things? Hm? What's the answer to that?'

'Well ... ahem ... brother ... I think you're asking a whole range of questions there that would be best answered in some private, one-to-one counselling. Perhaps if you could see me after the meeting we could arrange ... ', He made it sound like a threat, despite the smile. Several happy-clappy heavies were circling me now.

'Na – I don't think I'll bother. This Jehovah sounds like a parochial wee war god from the Middle East of a few thousand years ago. Gets embroiled in squabbles with other deities over the slightest wee thing, and we all have to suffer for it. Actually, I think it's about time that *He* asked our forgiveness for *His* sins. Or at least said sorry. And while we're about it – what happened to the world ending with the generation of 1914? Not many of them left now – hm? So when's it going to happen then? Hm?'

I was very pleased with myself. Wiped all the smug smiles off their smug faces. Then I saw you struggling to hold back the tears. You took Christina by the hand and fled. They all stared at me. I felt this small.

As I walked home that evening, I told myself I was just trying to show off. Then a while later I admitted to myself that I'd done it to hurt you, because I was jealous of your happiness, and your certainty, and the fact I wasn't the most important thing to you any more. Worst of all, when I thought back on my performance in the hall I realised I had sounded just like Dad.

You never really forgave me for that. I didn't ask for your forgiveness, of course, and I know you would've given it if I had, but … well, I just couldn't. If I had it would've meant acknowledging that there is a possibility that creepy George and all those other nutters are right – they are the meek who shall inherit the Earth. It doesn't bear thinking about.

But I'm saying it now. I'm sorry. I'm sorry I embarrassed you. I'm sorry I deceived you. I'm sorry for the lack of respect I showed for your feelings, if not your beliefs.

I really miss you. Not the you, now, so much. But the you then.

Maybe the world has ended. Maybe Armageddon happened while I was staggering around after seeing that girl slashed. Or maybe it all happened when I was shagging that bird in the flat. Or maybe it happened when she … when she …

Can you get mail in Paradise, I wonder?

32: A GHOST IN PARADISE

Stand still.
Avert your eyes from these beasts of the jungle
And their visceral venting of spleen

Bide time, all wrongs will be righted
All calumnies settled
They did you wrong – They'll get theirs

Be watchful
Be careful you don't falter
Or you could end up like me.

Forgiveness is easy when you're always right –
A black tear squirted from the face of the righteous angel.

You will sip
From the bounty of another Eden
Replenished, reborn, restored.

I will walk
Among the ashes of another Dresden
Howling, forsaken, alone.
Amid the ruins
I am walking, walking, walking.

I am your brother,
your sister,
your mother,
your father,
your daughter,
your husband,
your lover,
your son.

Amid the blackened, smouldering skies
Though reflected back in clear blue eyes
Of children carrying sins of old

I am walking ... walking ... walking ...
A ghost in your paradise

Bim bim

bom bom

Bom bom

bim bim

Chimes. Church. Clock.
I can hear it but I can't see it.
I wonder what time it is?
It must be …

One …

Two …

Three …

Four …

Five …

Five?

Five o'clock and all is well. Yeh right.

Five o'clock, though. That's another … what? God knows how many hours till daylight. Christ.

Jesus. I've … I … lost something … somewhere. I must've … I must've fallen asleep somewhere … sometime …

Some time. Lost. Gone. Forever. It must've been at … that flat. With Fifi and that … wee girl. Vivienne? Or …

Forget it. (and don't go there)

Just Forget it.

I've got to get home. Now. No more pissing about.

I've had enough of all this.

Just move.

Fuck … My feet are aching. They feel all pussed and blistered.

These shoes …

These shoes …

These fucking shoes. How the hell did I end up in these?

Funny thing, Time. If you travel along lines of longitude Time changes … it bends. With the curve of the earth or something. I think it bends and distorts at other times too. It's not just that sitting in a lecture or watching a wildlife programme on the telly or listening to Dad drone on about dialectic materialism that time seems to slow down – it actually does slow down. I'm sure of it. Why should it be that Time is consistent and perpetual and true? It could be like sound: Loud and sharp and slow and quiet and distant and near and pianissimo and infinitely varied and unique. Or it might ebb and flow like the weather. Why can't Time be like the wind? – breathless and humid and still, or fierce and wild and like a hurricane. And different in different places for different people.

I mean, the world can't even agree on a calendar. Oh, I know Pope Gregory introduced the popular one in 15 or 16-something, but lots of places still don't use it. The Muslims think it's only about 1400 and something. The world can't even agree what year it is, never mind what Time is.

That summer after I left school. I'd been looking forward to it so much – freedom from the tyranny of the school timetable and idiot teachers – but when it came … when it came, it was such a huge blank. It rained for the first week or so and I just lay in my room. Then it was sunny for a day or two, then it turned really sticky and hot and humid. The clamminess and mugginess seemed to settle on my brain and I just couldn't do … anything. I would lie on top of my bed for hours and hours at a time, not doing anything but staring into space. It was like I was barely conscious, a kind of waking coma, a nothingness. A nothing. A no-thing. I wouldn't let anyone into my room – it was the first time I'd really had it to myself since Steven had left for Police Training College. Mum just used to leave food outside the door. Sometimes I would eat it and sometimes I wouldn't. People would call round for me and I wouldn't see them, or if I did there would be no real conversation – just monosyllabic grunts from me. They stopped coming.

I thought about lots of things, and some of it seemed really profound and important but I can't remember a single bit of it now. Something about aliens watching us and different planes of existence – stuff like that. I forget it all now, though it seemed astounding then. The thing I do remember is staring at a little sliver of wire hanging down from the pelmet across the window. It was perfectly still but the longer I looked at it, everything else in the world just … faded away and it began to vibrate – almost imperceptibly at first then increasingly violent and wild. It wobbled and danced but still didn't really move. It was as if I was watching its very atoms moving. It mutated until there was thousands, millions of them oscillating around this axis. That's the only thing I can remember.

Sleeping and waking became the same thing. I kept the curtains closed. Day and night were meaningless. Dreaming seemed more real than real life, but even the dreams became uneventful. There was a clock in the room, my 'Baby Ben' alarm clock that used to try and rouse me for school every morning. The arms still went round the face but it meant nothing. Sometimes I would look at it, look away for a few seconds, look back and find six hours had passed. Other times I wouldn't look at it for hours and hours and find the arms hadn't moved. I didn't wind it, so it should have stopped, but it didn't. It just kept on going. Sometimes I would listen keenly for the 'tick tock' and be unable to hear it, even if I put my ear right to it. Other times it would be like

TICK TOCK

thudding like an amplified steamhammer in my brain. That's when I realised clocks don't work. Maybe they work mechanically or electronically or whatever – maybe – but as instruments of measuring time they're useless. Clocks and calendars – made up. Inventions of men that only mean something to men. Time cannot be measured. Time is immeasurable. Time is elusive, beyond, and – whisper it – may not even exist.

That summer, though. 'That summer!' should've been recalled with a slight ache of nostalgia for beach parties, candy floss girls who came across, and happy, carefree days spent drunk or stoned. That summer, for me,

Time stopped dead. I lay there until I atrophied and felt my skin turn to dust and my organs shrivel and decay. With my last vestige of being I pushed myself up from the floor and propelled myself from the room. I staggered out of the door and into the street. It was dark, which said it was night, but you can never be sure.

Next thing I knew I was standing on a platform waiting for a train. I was trying to breathe deeply, inhale the cool, clear air, but it was all flat and thick and smelt of fried onions and diesel. I got on a train. I don't know where it's going. I close my eyes in a tunnel and the chug of the engine recedes to a very small point. I try to open my eyes but I can't and I feel Time slowing down again, grinding to a halt. I want to scream but I can't move, not even my lips, and nothing comes out. I force my eyes to open and I'm blinded by the glare. I'm all alone. There's no one in the carriage. My head ratchets around, each microscopic movement an effort of will. Across the aisle my reflection stares back with wild, frightened eyes … a strange young lad no more than fourteen. A child's rubber ball bounces down the passageway. I turn back and my forehead rests against the glass and I peer through the blackness at the station approaching us at the speed of light. I'm still and everything else is moving, hurtling past me. My eyes jump back to focus on the blurred and jowly old man whose head meets mine on the other side of the pane. I'm somewhere in between, caught there, impaled on the arrow of Time while the train goes onward, ever onward. The scream builds, reaches a critical mass, and erupts, escaping like a force of nature. The guard on the platform hears my scream. It hits him at a thousand miles per hour. I only screamed it at thirty.

That's how I know Time is dead.

Now …

here ...

later ...

I ...

I ...

I think it's happening again.
I need to see another soul.

I need to know other people exist.

I need ...

I need ...

34: WINDOWS

Jesus Christ. Life.
Houses, not tenements.
Not flats.
Suburbia.
Must be reaching the edge of the city now.

God, help me, I'm hungry. Jesus, I'm starving. God! My
stomach! Bloated with hunger, I am, like an Ethiopian
refugee.

Skin and bone and a bloated belly.
Jesus.

Christ.

Jesus.

A light in a window.
Relief from the darkness.
Help me.

Please.

Please.

Nice lawn.

Nice garden.

Nice trees.

Nice people.

Live here.

Help me.

Help me.

Light.

French windows.

Help me, please.

No curtains.

A woman.

Help me, please.

A woman, dressing …

undressing …

in her living-room

through the French windows

takes off her skirt …

folds it …

takes off her blouse …

puts it on a hanger …
white skin burnished sun-lamp brown …

black underwear …

bra and pants …

black tights …

rolled down …

down …
revealing …

long …

fleshy …

white-brown …

thighs.

Sits down …

elongates her feet …

pulls her knees to her …

chest …

rolls the black tights off of her legs.

Stands up.

She's got big pearly glasses perched on her long nose.

Silver-gold hair …

long..

tinted, brushed and swept back …

just so.

She touches her face …

gently …

with her finger …

runs her hand under her chin and stretches the skin …

smoothing …

patting …

pulling …

defining.

Puts her hands behind her back and …

pushes her elbows out and …

arches her back and …

fiddles with the catch of her black bra and …

unfastens her black bra and …

holds the cups of her black bra and …

narrows her shoulders to let the straps fall off and …
lets the bra fall into her hands and …

places the bra over the back of the chair and …

pulls her chin into her chest so it disappears and …

lets her glasses slip down her nose and …

examines her pale white breast …

and her red-brown nipple …

handling it …

peering at it..

touching it …

feeling it …

brows knotted …

kneading it …

cupping it …

clinically …

frowning …

and …

looking up

and …

meeting my eyes …

and …

staring straight back into mine …

the windows of my soul …

her soul …

and …

'SCREEECH!'

No. Mrs. No. Don't …

Scream. I was just … I didn't mean to …

Please! Mrs! Please! I'm sorry!

I'm SORRY!

I didn't mean to …

I was just …

Oh God.

Oh help

Oh fuck

Oh run.

Oh fuck oh run.

Down here.

Over the fence.

Along the street.

Walkdontrunwalkdontrunwalkdontrun. Walk dontrun. Walk dontrun.

Walk don't run.

Walk don't run.

Walk, don't run.

Don't run.

Walk.

Calm.

Cool.

Don't bring attention to yourself.

You're just walking down this nice suburban street.

In the pishing rain.

In the middle of the night.

Nothing suspicious about that.

Walk.

DON't run.

Okay.

It's okay.

Polis.

meemaw meemaw meemaw

meemaw meemaw

meemaw meemaw

Oh fuck. Hide.

WHERE?

WHERE?

There.

A fast black hack: 'TAXI!'

35: TAXI (dermy)

'Go! Go! Go!' I'm shouting and off it goes, screeching away.

I'm gasping and panting and looking out the back window to see if the polis are following but the glass is shadowed, that kind of one-way mirror trick thing, and it's really hard to make out anything except the sulphurous blur of jaundiced street lights trailing orange ribbons of light in their wake. I try to swallow but my saliva feels thick and oily and my lungs feel like they've been burnt out in a forest fire.

Here, this fucking taxi's not half …

'Hey! You can slow down, mate, there's … '

No response.

'Hey! Mate! I said you can slow down a bit!'

This guy's just ignoring me.

'I SAID – HEY!! YOU CAN SLOW DOWN ARE YOU DEAF OR …'

I prod him. Nothing. It's a …

Dummy. A mannequin. A …

Oh God. Oh Jesus.

THERE'S NO ONE DRIVING!!!

And this thing's hurtling along like the fucking Formula One in Monaco and there's no one in the controls. But how the hell did it … ?

'Slow down.'

It slowed.

'Slow down further.'

It slowed again.

'Slow down to thirty miles per hour.'

Now I can't drive. I was supposed to get lessons for my Twenty-First birthday but … something happened. I can't remember. Anyway I can't drive. My Dad took me out once but we ended up arguing and that was the end of that. My total road driving experience therefore amounts to less than quarter of an hour with my Dad bawling in my ear on a country road behind Hamilton.

But this … thing, this … vehicle, it's … following my orders. It's getting me out of here. It's getting me away from this … hell-hole, this fucking nightmare. All I've got to do is guide it. Direct it. It is following my orders. I am in control. At last! I'm making some fucking headway home. I could take this all the way. I could take this right to the door. I could …

'Oh FUCK!!!!'

… right over a fucking mini-roundabout!!! Fucking hell!!! It's speeding up again too. Oh fuck. This is harder than I thought. This is …

'Go right! Go right! Turn right!!!'

Jesus. It just keeps going straight unless I tell it to …

'Left! Left!!! Go fucking LEFT!!!'

Fuck!!. My heart is pounding. It's fucking boom-boom-boom. Fuck this thing is getting fast and faster again, it's fucking …

… it's fucking copying me. Calm down. Slow down.

'Slow down.'

Calm down. Slow down.

'Slow down.'

It slows. Twenty-five miles per hour.

It slows. It does it. I lean forward and read the speedo. Twenty-five miles per hour.

This is weird. This reminds me of that time I was coming down from Thurso when I was hitching down for Uncle Robert's funeral and …

Fucking Hell! Violent swerve on the road! This is …

God. This needs everything. This needs all of my attention. I've got to focus on this. I can't take my mind off it for a second. This is …

Redlight: 'STOP!!'

THUMP! Heap on the floor. Ow. Oh. Aayah!

Green. 'Go forward. Slowly.'

It crawls off at about five miles per hour. Christ! This is fucking hard.

'Accelerate gently to twenty-five miles per hour.'

Got to think. Got to think. This could work. This could get me home. What if the polis stop me now? What am I going to say? How am I going to explain? Am I in charge of this vehicle? I am still drunk, or stoned, or both? Am I fit to be in charge of this vehicle?

'Well, I'm more fit than fucking Action Man here, officer.'

WHOAH!!!

Got to look where I'm going. Get a sense of where I am.

'Straight ahead, straight ahead, but take it easy.'

Somehow I know I'll have to pay for this. You always do. But I'm skint, broke, beam ends. I wonder … if I took it all the way home, maybe I could chap up the old man and get him to pay. I'll tell him I'll square up with him later. Yeh. All I need to do is direct it home. That's all.

I peek over the driver seat. Tap on the head of Parker in the front seat here. Plastic. Jesus???

What the fuck is going on here? Am I tripping or hallucinating or

Eyes on the road!!

Eyes on the road. It's just orange lights in a browny-black background. This is just a fucking blaze of streetlights in some fucking suburb and it could be anywhere. I could be anywhere. I am nowhere.

Oh, oh. Wait a minute. The meter – the meter is clocking up at a rate of knots: £29.75 … £29.85 … £29.95 … £30.00.

Thirty pounds! Christ! No way will the old man pay for this! I'll have to … I'll have to pay for this! Jesus!

It speeds up again.

'Slow down.'

Calm down, calm down. Got to get out. The Dummy won't, can't collect. There's nobody here. Nobody knows. Just get out. This is too fucking difficult anyway.

'Pull in to the side of the road and … '

It veers to the edge of the kerb, winging a parked motor on the way. Fuck!

I try to open the doors but they're locked. They won't open. They won't fucking open!

Got to get out of here. I can't take this.

Then I get it.

'Wait here for ten seconds then proceed slowly, following the road ahead.'

I jump out and leg it up the adjacent street. As soon as I'm out of sight I hear it start off again.

Thank God. Thank Christ.

Phew!

What's a fucking dummy doing driving a cab? What kind of a set-up is that?

Next thing I hear this screech of brakes and skidding tyres. I poke my head round the corner tentatively.

It's all over the fucking road! It's zig-zagging all over the fucking road, careering into parked cars and lamp-posts and …

Oh God. Oh no. It's going to hit that guy. It's going to …

'Noooooooooooooo!'

Too late. Oh Christ. Oh Hell. What have I done?

36: DEAR SIR

Dear Sir

    I'm soh … rry. I'm so fugging soh … rry. Jesus. God.
I'm so sorry. I'm so fugging sorry. I di'n't meen it. I jus …

    An now you're ded. I'm sorry. I'm so sorry. Wha can
I doo? Wha can I doo?

Oh fug.

Whad a mess.

Whad a fugging mess.

I'm so sorry.

Lemme ge yoo out of th fugging road.
Oh God. Pleese.

Hnnffff.

Hnnnnnnnffffffffffffffffffff.

Fugging dead weight.

Fugging dead man.

It wasn my fuggin fault.

I'm sorry.

It wasn my fault.

Fugging taxi.

Fuggin God-forsaken stupid fuggin taxi.
It wasn my fault.

Hhhhhhhhhhnnnnnnnnnnnnnnnnnnnnnnnnnnnnnnffff
fffffffffffffffffffff!!!!!!

Fugging move! (fucking bastard)
MOVE!!

Should've been fugging looking where you were fuggin goin!!

Fuggin drunken ol tramp!

Fuggin lush alkie ol bum!

No fugging wunder yoo got run over!!

No fugging wunder!

Fugging coat comin off now.
Fuggin coat.

Fuggin bastard.

Fuggin bastard coat.

I'm havin it!
I'm fugging cold and fugging wet and fugging freezing and
you're fugging dead so I'm havin the fugging coat! Right!

Right?!

Right.

Is mine. Fine.

I'm havin th fugging coat.

You're fuggin dead an I'm still fuggin alive an I'm fuggin freezin an my fuggin need's greater than yours 'cos you're fuggin dead an the Bible sez my need is greater than yours an you're fuggin ded so it dozen madder enymore but it'll help me get home.

Whad th fug ar yoo loogin ad?!

WHAD TH FUG AR YOO LOOGIN AT, CUNT?

Oh. Is me. In th win'doh. Shop win'doh. Burtin's win'doh. Tha's me. Fuggin Man at C&A. Fuggin Mizder Bow Jangles. Fuggin poncey fuggin cunt in the fuggin catalogue, pose … posin like a fuggin haddy.

Coo-eee!

Coo-eee, bloo-ee!

Oh you're fuggin byootefull.

I can … I can … I can imajin wha th ol cunt's gonny say when he sees me wearin this he'll say …

he'll say …

'yoo … yoo fugging waste of space. Whassat? Whassat yoo've got on? Is tha your new yooniform for yoor new fugging job as the village idiot!'

ha! Tha's wad e'll say.

Fuggin cunt.

Fukkinin cunt.

Yoo, yoo fukkinin dead cunt. Yoo don mind, d'yoo?

Eh?

D'yoo.

Fuggin Dad cunt.

Anyway …

I godda go.

I godda get home.

Then I'll go back to my bed an sleep for a month.

A year.

His shoos fit bedder than mine too, as well, an they're in one peece.

Time to move on.

Ged back.

Noht much father now.

Noht much.

Probbly.

37: ANOTHER COUNTRY

The final flickers of starlight on the horizon. And what a horizon. Dark, low hills huddled together like sleeping giants under a blanket, frozen together during the last ice age. Above them is the radiant sky, the black of night beginning its slow fade to the blue of morning. Wide open space with no puny artificial lights to relieve the great, smooth darkness. Only the stars, and the waning Moon.

The dying moments of the night in the minutes before sunrise in the valley of darkness.

No gaudy neon gaudy glare to corrupt the perfect vistas of dark rising up to the looming peaks of the rolling hills. No winking headlamps or dazzling diode or fabricated flashing filaments.

Just darkness.

Real darkness.

Pure darkness.

Relief from the tyranny of searching electric lights that only create shadows, and illuminate nothing. For once I'm glad my ginky eyesight doesn't give me sharp focus. I may not be able to read signs from a distance, but at least the sharp points of light don't jab at my eyes.

I could lose myself in here. In this valley of darkness.

I fear nothing in this valley of darkness, for I have walked through that darker valley: The seething, serpentine streets of the city.

At last ... it is behind me. I am free of its clinging, leeching air; of its rotting, retching streets; of its decrepit, derelict towers, its bilious, belching buildings. I am free.

I am free. Free to be me again. Free in this valley, this valley of darkness, this valley of light, this valley of ...

In this valley lies my home.

Somewhere in this dark pool, it lies ... sleeping. Waiting.

This is another country. A foreign land. A foreign land I call home, for want of something else.

The past is another country. I read that somewhere, once. At school? At university? Can't remember. Who said it? David Hume? Nah. Shakespeare? Maybe. A poet? A poem from school? A book, maybe. I don't know. I can't remember. Dad might know. Then again, maybe not. Someone though. Someone knows.

If the past is another country, I'm still adrift on an island betwixt and between. Washed up on a desolate, rocky place with continents of past distant, unreachable, and untouchable. Untouchable. I am untouchable. I cannot touch.

But in these other states, I am the citizen of many nations.

To that woman on holiday in Millport many, many years ago, I am that cheeky wee boy who skooshed her in the face with my water pistol. And in her nation, I am only him.

To that bloke I pushed down the stairs at the Apollo after the Clash concert, I am that bastard who broke his leg. And in that nation, I am only him.

To that girl I sat beside on the bus as we watched the cow die, I am the ignoramus against which she may measure herself when she recounts that story. And in her nation, I am only that.

In the nation of that once beautiful woman whose face is now forever scarred, I am nothing but the coward who let her down, who ran away.

In the nation of Jakesie, I am that little bastard he never quite caught up with, the one who got away.

And in the nation of Fi-fi, left holding her baby, I am … what? A … a … What? A What? A … what am I? Who am I to her?

Nothing. Nobody.

Nothing.

It's all in the past. Another country. Another state.

For now I am here.

But I long for places far, far away.

I long for that frowsy little bedsitter flat where I lay with Vivienne, touching her white, naked body, stroking her dark, lustrous hair, kissing her sweet, red lips.

I ache for that warm, cosy hearth, huddled to my mother, watching the flames on the fire dance while the snow beat down outside.

I yearn for the mattress of fresh cut grass and my laughter as my father throws me into the heap and I land softly after a moment of fear and I hear his hearty bellow and feel his strong arms as he picks me up again. I want to blink against the sun and bathe in the happiness and security of his love.

He did love me once. On that isle of the past, he loved me once. And I knew it.

Far distant, far distant. The other side of the world.

If the past is another country, the future is another planet, another galaxy – a swirling, billowing mass of dust and atoms, never fully formed, still moving beneath your feet as you step onto it. And then it is an island, an isthmus to another continent of nations of the past, each warring with the other in a seething civil conflict that never ends.

I need to get off this island. I am Robinson Crusoe, with no Friday, Saturday or Sunday. I am Gulliver without the Lilliputians or Brobdingnagians. I am a starving, withering shipwreck in need of a rescue. I want out.

And it's pissing down.

Fuck!

If I don't get a fucking move on I really will be on a fucking island.

I'm going to get soaked!

This is getting really heavy.

As if I'm not fucking cold enough already, fucking freezing ice cold rain starts lashing my face and …

FUCK!

… dripping down the back of my neck!

Fuck it. Fuck.

I'm f-f-f-f-fucking f-f-f-f-ffreeezing!

And Tomorrow is tantalisingly, teasingly close. And yet, I might never get there.

I need a ferry to tomorrow.

But who pays the ferryman?

38: DEAR DAD (again)

Dear Dad

I'm s-s-orry. I'm s-sorry. I'm s-s-so sorry for what I've b-b-become. I'm sorry for what I've done. I'm s-s-s-so s-s-sorry.

It's me again. I just wanted to say I'm s-sorry. I understand now. Y-Y-Y-You're not t-t-to blame for everything that's happened to m-me. Y-Y-You're not to b-blame for everything I am. You're not to b-blame at all.

I d-don't know how that guy died. He was just l-l-lying there. It's all haz-z-z-zy.

Yes, I know it's me that's being hazy. J-Just listen for a minute, will you. Please.

It's just th-that … I honestly can't remember. Everyth-th-thing just seems to be little s-s-spots and b-b-blotches of things that have happened, like a m-movie with no plot, just a j-jumble of images. I can't seem to make s-sense of it at all.

I kn-know I sh-shouldn't have t-taken his c-clothes. I'm s-sorry. I was c-cold.

So c-cold.

There's ice in the m-marrow of my bones. I c-c-c-c-can't s-s-s-s-s-stop sh-sh-sh-sh-shaking.

Please Dad. Please h-help m-me. I'm s-so cold. And it's all s-soft and s-squelchy underf-foot. I th-think I'm s-s-sinking. It's all boggy. Like a marsh.

It is a marsh.

That explains it.

I'm s-sinking in a boggy marsh.

I've found myself here … on my knees. Involuntary, but on my knees – here, in the middle of this sodden bog, in the black, pouring rain, wearing a dead man's clothes, arms akimbo like a scarecrow in a field even the birds wouldn't want, lost and alone, sinking deeper, and deeper into the mud.

And suddenly I can remember good things about you. For all those years I could only remember – only *wanted* to remember all the little cruelties, all the small indignities, all the long silences.

I'd forgotten all the kindnesses. Taking me swimming in the loch on holiday. Playing football in the park with me and my mates. Coming to watch me on Saturday mornings in the pissing rain when I played for the school team. Helping me with my maths homework because I could never do it. But you could.

I just felt like you contained me. I was so like you. Everyone said so. I was your spitting image. 'You're your Dad's double,' they would all say. And they were right. I am you. A squandered, slothful shadow of you, but you all the same. That's why I've blown it. That's why I went against everything you said. I was trying to be me when there was no me to be.

I know you tried to help me, but it's too late.

I did want to make you proud, but it's too late.

I just wish you could hold me in your arms right now. Or throw me up into that stack of cut grass again, laughing and smiling and shaking.

Sh-shaking.

I'm so cold now, Dad. I don't know if I'm going to make it.

I'm sorry. I'm so sorry.

I know you were only trying to do your best.

Sincerely,

Your Son.

39: MARSHLANDS

This is it then. Sinking slowly into a marshy bog. Already its icy liquids are seeping through my shoes and creeping up my legs and pulling me

down, down, down, down onto my knees. Now it's slithering and sliming over my knees and soon it will pull me

down, down, down and lap past my chest, my shoulders, my neck, my mouth, my nose, my eyes, my head, my hair, until I am gone. No more. Gobbled back up to the Earth that begat me and …

Oh. It appears to have stopped.

Still. I can't seem to move.

Fine.

Great.

I'll just wait here till the sun comes up and sooner or later

somebody will happen past and

rescue me.

Rescue me.

Please.

Somebody.

Someone.

Something.

I'm so c-c-c-c-c-c-c-cold.

I'm so c-c-c-c-c-c-c-c-c-c-c-c-c-c-c-c-c-c-c-c-o-o-o-o-o-o-o-o-o-l-l-l-l-l-l-l-d-d-d.

P-p-p-p-please God. Help me.

I'll be good.

I promise.

Please. Help me.

Get me out of here.

Do something.

Come on!

Something!

Surely an omnipresent, omnipotent entity like you can pull something out of the hat for a simple wee job like getting me out of this boggy shithole.

Come on!

Typical. So I've just to freeze to death here in this stinky, smelly, squelchy, sodden bog, then?

Fine. Have it your way. You know best.

!Crack!

Oooh! Thunder and lighting.
Nice touch.

40: DEAR ...

Dear ...

(Jehovah Allah Yahweh YHWH HaShem Vishnu Mother Nature Sat Guru Ra Jupiter Jove Zeus Jesus Jah Supreme Being. Whatever.)

You know who you are. It's just us idiots who don't know. Oh, we make some guesses, then dress it up as the Truth, but really – we haven't got a clue.

I remember we had a Geography teacher ... or was he a Physics teacher ... whatever, we had this teacher. It was Physics. Anyway, he was pretty good. Mr Plumb was his name. The kind of name you'd make a joke of normally and ... well, we did make jokes about his name. But that wasn't the point you see, because he was a good teacher. Yes, I know most people don't believe in such figures anymore, preferring to say they're just myths and legends, but he actually was one. In fact he was great. People never cut his classes. And he wasn't a joker or an eccentric or one of those guys who tried to be your friend or let you away with everything, he was actually quite strict, but he never seemed to have to raise his voice. He was just average height, mousy hair starting to go thin and grey, and he always wore a lab coat with acid burns and stains on it. But he was a great man because he didn't talk down to you and he didn't ignore your questions and he made everything so ... clear. Everybody understood him. Everyone knew what he was on about. Everybody listened to him.

One day I remember him explaining about the formation of the Earth's atmosphere. I don't think it was part of the curriculum as such, not that such things bothered Mr Plumb. Anyway he was describing the big bang theory and the ever-expanding universe and the speed of light and the evolution of star systems and the establishment of our solar system. And all this to a third year class. When he was talking

about it, his eyes lit up and you were captivated. All of us.
Even the skullcrushers at the back of the room. I know this
because I can still remember what he was talking about that
afternoon. He said that the conditions for life on Earth are
unique, that there's this fantastically unlikely configuration
of circumstances – gases, water, DNA, all that stuff – and that
it was quite possible we are the only carbon-based life form
existent in the entire universe. Well. That begged a question.
Somebody asked it. 'Does that mean you're saying there are
other forms of life in the universe, sir? Aliens?'

'Of course,' says old Plumb. 'But not like us.
Nothing like us. Perhaps they exist in a way that we could
not even perceive.'

There was a stunned silence. Teachers didn't say
things like that. Alien life forms on other planets we couldn't
even perceive if they were standing in front of our eyes?
Surely not. But yes, that's exactly what he was saying.

The moment passed and he did this drawing on
the blackboard showing the Earth like a goldfish bowl, with
all the necessary ingredients there in the correct proportions
required to sustain life. It was astonishing. Another question
begged. Somebody asked it. It was me. I said:

'Do you think there's a God then, sir.'

'I don't know,' he said. 'Nobody does. We all just
kind of hope there is. We just hope this isn't all a big pointless
coincidence.'

I persisted. 'But like in the Bible, sir? God like that.'

'One who cares about every indignity and dilemma
going on in the world? No, I doubt it.' He raised his eyebrows
and stared out of the window for a moment. 'But maybe He
is there … watching. Watching us through the glass of our
atmosphere, lit by the reflection of the Sun. Maybe that's
how he's watching us.'

And that's how I began to think of You. As this
disinterested celestial scientist, gazing down at us from time
to time, observing how we get on with things, making a few

notes, then turning away for another few millennia to check on some other little hothoused lifeforms scurrying around their globe.

It was all there in Plumb's eyes. One of the only people I ever really thought was worth listening to – he thought it was all just some arcane, unknowable experiment. Worthwhile to some greater purpose, perhaps, but as significant and disposable to You as a slide of cells under a microscope was to him.

So here I am, an infinitesimally small fragment of one of Your lesser experimental planets among the millions of others, struggling for a few nanoseconds of the eternity You set to run these things on. But I want Your attention. Just for a minute.

I thought I saw Your face just now. Just as the daylight began to break over the backs of those big hills. I saw You. All of a sudden … just as it was ready to be a bright sunny day … these dark blue clouds surged up above the horizon and I saw Your face in them. Peering through the precipitation, You, Your face, glancing down at the microbes below. Your impassive countenance framed by a mass of curls that may have been clouds, but could have been your hair. You looked like You were making notes. Then I blinked – or You did – and You were away. Gone. On to the next one.

But You were beautiful. Not in a specific, handsome way, but beautiful. Awe-inspiring, mind-blowingly beautiful.

Hey! Behold the Godhead! Gaze upon its beauty and weep! Contemplate its grace and wonder!

No. Not quite.

You were there and then You were gone. A glimpse … a momentary flash – no. Not even a moment. A fraction of … Time. But unforgettable. Indelible.

Time. That old one. That's one of your best tricks. Folding in on itself in ever-decreasing fractions.

I suppose that's why churches have clocktowers –

they proclaim their absolute certainty of Time, in the way they proclaim absolute certainty about God. And clocks are to Time what religions are to God – a self-referential design, a symbol of something to suggest order and certainty in a world beyond chaos. But of immense practical use for creating a concentrated consensus people will fear and obey. Of course, having achieved that, the assumption is made, or asserted, that the symbol is that which it merely represents, when it has, at best, only a tangential connection to the reality it claims to be.

But …

But …

Yes. I need Your help.

Yes, I am weak.

Yes, there is so much I don't know … I don't understand.

Please. Hear this plea. Read this letter.

Sincerely,

Well … you know who I am.

P.S.

Something is wrong and it's all wrong and everything is wrong and I don't know what but. Everything is wrong. Everything I thought I was, has gone and everyone I've ever known, I've used. I've stripped away everything and everything and there's nothing left. There is nothing. There is no me. I'm at the end, God. I've done some terrible thing … I've done some terrible things … and I … I … I can't … I can't even see them myself. And I'm so cold. I'm so-oo-oo-oo cold. I'm shivering and freezing and my t-t-t-t-t-teeth won't s-s-s-s-stop cha-cha-chattering. My skin feels all cold and slimy and puckered. My feet are like potatoes rotting in my boots. I can't even …

Please help me. Please help me get back. Send me a sign. Please. Send me a sign. Help me.

41: COUNTRY ROADS
(TAKE ME HOME)

And suddenly …

I'm wading out of it. It's clinging to me like black oily limpets, but I'm wading through it and I'm plodding out and …

THERE!!

YES!!

It's there!

A road I recognise. Full of fucking puddles and pools of water, but the road that leads to the road that leads to McGregor's Farm that sits on the outskirts of town. The town that is home.

I AM HERE!

YES!!

I am almost THERE!

Another half an hour … or so … and I'll be home!

YES! YES! YES! YES! YES!

YOU BEEZER, YOU FUCKING BRAMMER – FUCKING YES!

FUCKING UNBE*LIEVE*ABLE!!

I'VE MADE IT!

(*Loudly, with gusto*)
'Cunt'ry roads ... take me home
To the play-ace ... I bee-law-eee-ong!
West Vir-jin-ya ... Mountaina Ma-Ma-aah
Take-a me hoe-mmmm ...
Cun-tree row-oh-d-sah ...

Take me hoe-mmmm ...
Cun-tree row-wa-ah, ow-wa-ah, ow-wa-ah, ow-wa-ahds ...'

Here, wait a minute.
I don't remember ...

42: DEAD LETTER HOUSE

that.

Yet ...

(You recognise it) but not specifically.

(Try to remember) I knew this place ... once. These roads, this country, but ... this doesn't quite fit. But then again ...

it does. Sort of.

It's difficult to see through that curtain of rain.

I peer at it for a long, long time.

(I thought it was a castle at first. A towered fortress erupting from the ground imbued with the anger of ancient volcanoes. Exuding strength and invulnerability to those who would dare to breach its walls)

But ... no. It's not that ... exactly.

(I thought it was a church, a medieval monument to faith, built by men in a society of secrets, determined to institute an icon of order in defiance of the brutal chaos they saw all around them. A towering point to cast men's eyes heavenwards, away from the grubbing, filthy dirt of the earth, to inspire and to engender aspiration. A great finger pointing beyond the petty concerns of the now, to the hope for a better eternity)

But ... no. It's not that ... exactly.

(Then it was a ruin ... a tumbling, disgraced collection of mighty stones hewn from mightier rocks. Scattered clusters of cornerstones, climbing to jagged spikes, clinging to the dignity that once they were walls, but the holes in the fabric of their facades suggesting more than just lost fenestration)

But ... no. It's not that ... exactly.

That murky grey light of dawn that threatened has

disappeared once more. The light drowned by black clouds and black rain. It was as if the sun had strained to clamber over the horizon, but was beaten back down by these agents of darkness and night. The night isn't finished yet.

Nor is the rain.

This storm's really letting loose now.

Do I … ? Or do I go on?

Mmmmm.

Go on?

Or go in?

Go in.

Enter …

this …

this …

House. It is.

A Mansion House. Not a ruin. Not … exactly.

Windows … black, but intact. High, arched, latticed glass. Revealing nothing. Giving nothing away.

I approach … it seems to solidify. Now it looks … real … tangible. Solid. Little turreted walls on top of the protuding bay windows. Walls … broader and deeper than high. I can't really see how deep it is. This is only the façade. Maybe it is only a façade.

But it's like …

like …

it's drawing me to it. Breathing me in.

Promising shelter from this storm.

Chap the door. It's large and black and wooden and arched, with wrought iron hinges on weathered oak. Formidable. Ancient. Forbidding. This large, ringed handle is cold to the touch. Freezing. It's cold and wet but I'm colder and wetter.

So I pull back the ring and … try to chap the door with it. It won't make contact. It's too stiff. Not as stiff as me, though. Creaking joints and frozen fingers and …

It swings open.

I fall inside.

I'm inside.

It's dark. Completely dark. An all-enveloping dark. There's no way back so I lie here, face down, not daring to breathe. I feel the blood rushing to my head I can hear my heart beating. I can feel it pulsating, pumping blood all around me.

It feels like that's all there is in the world … this thudding, beating drum. But I'm warm. After the cold, the rain, the mud, the fatigue … this is everything: Warmth, comfort, shelter. I am safe.

I want to sleep. I'm so tired and it's so warm and I want to sleep. Please let me sleep.

Just listen to that pulse.

In this darkness, this perfect, complete darkness, I can't tell if my eyes are open or shut. I can't move. It's as if I have no body. No limbs, no mouth, no ears, no eyes. No nothing. A no-thing. I am a no-thing. Except, maybe, a beating, pumping heart, torn from its ribs, lying in this place. It's everywhere. It's all around me. It's all the blood pumping, it's

not me.

It's the House.

The House is pulsating.

It's …

Breathing.

Be still.

Be quiet.

Be.

Be …

A some-thing.

My legs curl up to my chest, and my arms pull them close to me. I tuck my head down between my knees. My heart thumping in my ears. In my brain. I shut my eyes, tight, preserving the darkness. The darkness recedes. Somewhere – I can sense it – there is light. Still huddling myself close, I see …

I saw …

I see …

a crack of light. A crack of light to let a draught of air in – insinuating, swirling, its wispy fingers stroking me, caressing me, pulling me out … pulling me towards the light. Part of me doesn't want to go. Part of me wants just to stay here forever. But another part of me, a part hardly known to me, but for once in the ascendancy is drawn to the light.

I stretch out and push and pull and crawl my way towards the light. The crack's getting bigger. The door's opening. I'm getting nearer.

I am afraid.

What's going to be on the other side? I don't want to know.

Yet still I claw and wriggle and slide towards that door. Towards that light. And then

Suddenly …

I am there. In this brightness. Dazzling brightness.

'God!'

I try to shield my eyes, but the light's too strong. It's like it's burning through my arm, through my eyelids, through the membrane, burning the back of my cornea.

Too strong.

Too much.

Please.

Stop.

I can't take it.

I'm begging you.

I'm on my knees, I'm …

I blink them open.

I'm kneeling on a hard wood floor, my eyes watering, overflowing, trying to focus on what's before me.

Colours blur and swirl before me –

it's Jackson Pollock … it's Picasso … it's Van Gogh … it's … it's …

Rembrandt.

I'm kneeling on a hardwood floor (my knees are aching, get up off your knees) in a grand hall. Countless crystal chandeliers dangle from the ceiling high above me. Rounded walls roll out on either side – the room is vast ... circular. Elliptical. Gold leaf, Greek statues and Gargoyle heads ... everywhere. Opulent. Decadent. Like an entrance hall to a great theatre, except ...

Except ...

There are doors. All along the walls, tier upon tier of doors reaching up

Up

Up

Up

Up to a

high, domed ceiling, so high it (hurts my neck) hurts my neck to look at it.

And before me ... a grand staircase dominates the room – a huge, epic, sweep that splits into spirals after the first landing, a double set of spiral stairs twirling up and up and up and ... it makes me feel sick just looking at them. They seem to go on forever.

I stare back at the main stair, into a blood-red carpet, the banister a series of pillars shaped like ... like ...

Hourglasses.

No. They're not shaped like them – they are hourglasses. Each step flanked by a bulbous figure eight, sands tumbling through them but ... all at different rates. All at different rates.

What is this place?

I hear voices ... distant, far away – strange, unintelligible voices, speaking strange dialect. Suddenly colours and noise career around me, like a carousel.

Music!

Wondrous, sonorous music. It's ... it's ... so beautiful. It fills me, rises up inside of me – a fountain of ululating, chanting voices. Ecstatic song of such joy ... such life ... it seems to be all around me, it seems to be coming from deep inside of me ... it lifts me up off of my knees and I feel so light, so full of this incredible music, like it's going to lift me right up to the ceiling, like I can fly, like I'm ...

I'm ...

I'm standing on my own two feet. The hall is filling with people! Noisy, chattering people dressed in black dinner suits and white silk ballgowns. They're dancing, waltzing, around me and more and more of them pour out of ... somewhere ... under the stairs ...

pouring out ...

a multitude ...

hundreds of them ...

Dancing.

But ...

but ...

but they're not dancing to the music I can hear. They're all out of time, out of sync. They're not even listening, they're just careering about, crashing into one another and ... laughing. And chattering. Talking. Blethering. They're not listening to the music at all. All I can hear is their silly voices and ... they've all got masks on. White alabaster masks where their faces should be – eyeless, no holes for nostrils but with smiling, animated mouths – laughing, talking, chattering, singing but no expression on their faces, their death mask faces. Just mouths moving constantly, noisily, drowning out the music. I can't hear the music anymore. I've lost the music. I can see it ... feel its echoes floating away, swallowed by this cacophony of silly, senseless chatter.

I cover my ears but I can't remember it. I can't even remember how it felt. I can only feel its absence. A hollow in my breast, a dullness in my head, fed by this buzz of gibberish from these faceless ...

They've stopped. It's silent. No talking, no dancing. They're all looking at me, like ... like ... I don't know what because they're all just white masks. But their mouths are still and quiet now.

A man in a surplice steps out of the crowd. He doesn't have a mask. He looks normal. He produces a camera from under the folds of his garment and ...

FLASH

Oh God. I can't see. Millions of coloured little flashbulbs spinning around. I stumble about. I feel sick. I'm falling ...

falling ...

falling ...

I blink my eyes open and they've all gone.

I am alone.

All alone.

I blink open my eyes and rub them.

I'm on the stairs. A light breeze flickers across my face. I blink again.

Where did they all go?

I clamber up the stairs ...

'HELLO!'

Nothing.

'HELLO-O-Oh!'

Nothing. Nobody there.

Where did they all go?

I clamber up the stairs. There must be somebody here. Somebody I can talk to.

Somebody I can explain to. Explain why I'm here. Somebody.

Whoa! These stairs are steep! I'm exhausted. I collapse on the floor of the landing and look around. No doors on this floor. Just spiral staircases looping up from every part of the landing. One of them must go somewhere. I'm going to find out. Let's see ...

White Black
Blue Red
Head Feet
First Last
Post Script
Writer Read
Only Just
Cause Effect
Pose Nude
Woman Man
Alive Dead
Centre Point
Blank Face
Facts Lie
Low High
Church Bell
Ring Road
Rage War
Peace Talk
Talk Sense
Fear Death
Valley Dolls
House Call
Home Sweet
Jesus Christ
Almighty Father
Mother Love
Hate Mail
Shot Down
Deep Sea
Salt Mines
Yours Truly
Oh God.

This is higher than I thought.
Don't look down.
(don't) **DON'T!!**

Oh God.   Oh Jesus.

Got to get ... (oh God) ... away from ... (Oh God)

... here. A door ... a door ...

... will do ...

Only one choice ...

I throw myself inside and slam it shut behind me.

Heart thumping.

Brow lashing sweat.

But ...

This is a blizzard.

I'm in a ...

Vast, vast room ...

... like a huge cinema, but ... raked upwards. To a distant point. And no seats. It's colossal. I can't ...? There's ... there ... seems to be a dim light at the other end of this ... but it's ... it's miles away. This vast auditorium is like ... the width of a city.

Jesus. Not another one.

A blizzard is blowing ... (jesus) everywhere. It's falling ... everywhere.

Walk on.

This ground is wet and sticky. Hey, this isn't ...

It's not snow. It's ... paper. Millions – billions – of tiny bits of white paper barrelling down from ... well, the sky? I don't know. I can't see it. It's everywhere. And in the distance ...

Shadows. Shadows scurrying through the hail of paper. Shadows grabbing at the flakes of paper as they fall. Shadows sifting through mounds of flecked paper. Paper sludge lying in great drifts in the contours of the floor.

This stuff is sticking to me. I'm going to be a snowman in a few minutes if I don't keep moving.

Keep moving.

At least it's solid ground.

God, this is getting thicker ...

That dim light in the distance ... it's ... a bit brighter. But ... my ears. And there's a deep hum, a deep buzzing, getting louder and louder and …

A shadow bumps into me.

'Sorry!' He laughs. 'Sorry, old man!'

I squint through the blizzard. Who is this guy?

'Who are you?'

'What?!'

'Who ARE you?!' I shout.

'I'm a helper!' he yells back at me.

'Oh. What are you helping with?'

'This!' And he shows me a sack full of the bits of paper. He smiles at me like I'm supposed to understand.

'Oh, right. What's this?'

'I'm sorry?'

I try again, louder. 'WHAT'S THIS?'

He looks at me idiotically. He's beginning to annoy me, this guy.

'Are you new?' he asks.

'I … not exactly. Well, maybe. I suppose so.'

'What?'

'I SUPPOSE SO!'

'Oh right.' He looks around him, like he'd like someone else to come and deal with me, like he's mildly irritated, like he can't be bothered explaining this to me, like *I'M* the idiot. Cheeky get.

'Look,' he says, pulling out another sack from his belt, 'just gather up as much as you can and make your way to the front. Okay?' He pushed the sack into my hands and stalks away grabbing handfuls of paperflakes as he goes. I shrug and grab a few for myself, stuff them into the sack and walk towards the feeble (but constant) light in the distance.

What a life. What a dull job. What did he do to end up here?

Ow! These little bastard bits of paper can cut you. That one just glanced off my cheek.

OW! One of the bits of paper's flown into my eye. Ah! That was sore!

I pick it out and look at it.

It's a photograph.

A portrait.

A tiny little photo of a face. A black face. A wee boy's face. African by the look of him. Smiling. Just his face and head. No shoulders. No background. Just his face.

I dab another one with my fingertip. It's a face too. An Asian girl. About fourteen.

Another. An Asian man – old. Geriatric.

Who are these people?

What's all this about?

I grab a handful from the floor and rake through them. They're all faces. Photographs of people's faces. What the fu …?

'**Hey!**' I spy another one of the shadows working close by me. 'Hey, you!'

He turns around. He's older than the first guy, wearing a hood, a kind of duffle coat or cassock. He's wearing spectacles and he smiles and nods as I approach him.

'Hello, my friend.'

Hmmm. Friendly type. 'Yeh, hi. I, ehm, I was just wondering … ' I dab one of the photos from the air and show it to him. 'These are all faces of people.'

'Yes.' He smiles. And nods.

'Mmm. Well, I was just wondering … '

'Yes?'

'… are they real people?'

'Yes. Of course!' He smiles and nods again and then turns back to his work.

He looks a bit dim, but I persist. I run up and tap him on the shoulder.

'Yes?'

'Look, I'm sorry if I appear a bit dense here, but what is all this about? Where do all these things come from? What are they for?'

He smiles and nods at me again. He's really

beginning to get on my wick, this guy.

'Why are we doing this?' I ask again.

'Ah … ' he says, smiling and nodding and walking away. I'm left – speechless. How fucking rude can you get!

Oh. He turns and beckons me with his hand. Evidently I'm meant to follow him.

We walk through the blizzard, me with my head down and eyes like slits against the howling wind and sharp paper cuts, him with his head up, still grabbing and scooping handfuls as he toddles along.

Weirdo.

After a moment or two he comes to a halt and I walk into his back.

'Sorry.'

He smiles. 'It's alright, my friend.' He turns and nods towards the light. 'That's what it's for.'

It's a massive screen – a sheer wall, so high you can't see the top, so broad you can't see the sides … overwhelming, but with the sense that somewhere out of sight it curves and creates a big wraparound cinemascope. I look back at the nodder blankly.

'That's where we put them all.' He says by way of explanation.

I shake my head. I'm obviously missing something here.

'Put what?'

'The faces. Those photographs are the faces of everyone.'

'Everyone?' I can feel my eyes gaping. He nods. And smiles. 'Everyone.' I think for a moment. 'Everyone who?' He frowns. Well, that's something. 'I'm sorry I still don't get it, mate.'

He tuts and tries again, talking slowly as if to a child – or an idiot – and pointing at the light on the screen for emphasis. 'We collect the photos, bring them to the front, and our brothers paste them to the screen.'

'Yes … but why?'

'To see the face of God.'

My jaw swung open.   'Are you serious?'

His face crumples slightly. I think he might be a bit offended. 'Of course,' he says, a little haughtily.

'And these photos, they're … '

'Everyone.' He confirmed.

'Everyone who, though? Everyone you know? Everyone I know? Everyone else? Everyone alive? Everyone who ever lived?'

'Everyone.'

'And once you've gathered them all and pasted them to this screen, you'll … '

'See the face of God.'

We pause, looking at each other.

I hand him my sack.

'Best of luck, mate.'

He says something as I turn away, but I decide to whistle to drown him out. Hey ho.

I look up at the screen: It's just a muddle of grey and black and white. A messy mosaic of monochrome madness. But maybe … just maybe a hint of a jawline …

'NA-AAH!'

I whistle a merry tune awhile, grateful I'm not one of those guys.

As I go they stumble past me, these shadows, grasping at the air, scrabbling on the ground, shovelling these little bits of paper into their sacks.

I push through the blizzard and find a door. I'm completely disorientated now … this could be the door I came in … then again …

Hmm. What to do, what to do.

I watch some of these loonies leaping about grabbing at the air. I go through the door.

Oh hell.

Clocks. Everywhere.

tick tock tick to ‹ tick tock tick tock tick tock tick tock tick tock tick tock tick
tock tick tock tic tock tick tock tick tock tick tock tick tock tick tock tick tock
tick tock tick tocl 'ick tock tick tock tick tock tick tock tick tock tick tock tick
tock tick tock tick ɔck tick tock tick tock tick tock tick tock tick tock tick tock
tick tock tick tock ɔk tock tick tock tick tock tick tock tick tock tick tock tick
tock tick tock tick t ˑk tick tock tick tock tick tock tick tock tick tock tick tock
tick tock tick tock ti ‹ tock tick tock tick tock tick tock tick tock tick tock tick
tock tick tock tick to ˑ tick tock tick tock tick tock tick tock tick tock tick tock
tick tock tick tock ticl 'ock tick tock tick tock tick tock tick tock tick tock tick
tock tick tock tick tocl ick tock tick tock tick tock tick tock tick tock tick tock
tick tock tick tock tick ˑck tick tock tick tock tick tock tick tock tick tock tick
tock tick tock tick tock ι ˑk tock tick tock tick tock tick tock tick tock tick tock
tick tock tick tock tick t. k tick tock tick tock tick tock tick tock tick tock tick
tock tick tock tick tock ti ˑtock tick tock tick tock tick tock tick tock tick tock
tick tock tick tock tick toc tick tock tick tock tick tock tick tock tick tock tick
tock tick tock tick tock tick ock tick tock tick tock tick tock tick tock tick tock
tick tock tick tock tick tock 'ck tick tock tick tock tick tock tick tock tick tock
tock tick tock tick tock tick ι ck tick tock tick tock tick tock tick tock tick tock
tick tock tick tock tick tock t. k tick tock tick tock tick tock tick tock tick tock
tock tick tock tick tock tick to 'k tick tock tick tock tick tock tick tock tick tock
tick tock tick tock tick tock tic tock tick tock tick tock tick tock tick tock tick
tock tick tock tick tock tick toc. tick tock tick tock tick tock tick tock tick tock
tick tock tick tock tick tock tick ɔck tick tock tick tock tick tock tick tock tick
tock tick tock tick tock tick tock ck tick tock tick tock tick tock tick tock tock
tick tock tick tock tick tock tick t. ˑk tick tock tick tock tick tock tick tock tick
tock tick tock tick tock tick tock ti ˑtock tick tock tick tock tick tock tick tock
tick tock tick tock tick tock tick to ˑ tick tock tick tock tick tock tick tock tick
tock tick tock tick tock tick tock tic. tock tick tock tick tock tick tock tick tock
tick tock tick tock tick tock tick tocl ick tock tick tock tick tock tick tock tick
tock tick tock tick tock tick tock tick ɔck tick tock tick tock tick tock tick tock
tick tock tick tock tick tock tick tock ˑ ˑˑ˙k tick tock tick tock tick
tock tick tock tick tock tick tocl   ˑtick tock tick tock
tick tock tick tock tick tock ˑ Fat ones,   'ˑ tick tock tick
tock tick tock tick tock ti   ˑk tick tock
tick tock tick tock tick   thin ones, big ones,   tock tick
tock tick tock tick to'   small ones, grandfathers,   'ˑk tock
tick tock tick tock t˙   grandmothers, pendulums, potatoes,   ˑk tick
tock tick tock tick   cuckoos, carriages, brackets, candles,   tock
tock tick tock tick   sundials, water, caesium, automata,   tick
tick tock tick tocl   ock
tock tick tock ticl   astronomic, astrologic, digitals, turret,   tick
tick tock tick tock   chronometers, escapements, fobs   ock
tock tick tock tick   tick
tick tock tick tock t   and chimes. They all tick different,   .tock
tock tick tock tick to   and tell different times, and   ˑk tick
tick tock tick tock tick   .ck tock
tock tick tock tick tock tι   they're all going to drive   .tock tick
tick tock tick tock tick tock .   me out of my ...   ˑk tick tock
tock tick tock tick tock tick tocɴ .   ˑ ˑˑˑ ˑtick tock tick
tick tock tick tock tick tock tick tock tιcн   . ˑ ˑ. ˑk tick tock tick tock
tock tick tock tick tock tick tock tick tock tick tick ti ˑ ˑtick tock tick tock
tick tock tick tock tick tock tick tock tick tock tick tock tick tock tick tock tick
tock tick tock tick tock tick tock tick tock tick tock tock tick tock tick tock

mind.

I'm none the wiser.

At least I can see another door out of here.

The door. A polished, light oak in a styled, rectangular frame. A tarnished brass handle. I turn it. Go through.

The lights go out instantly. Everything's silent. Everything's dark ... Maybe ...

... as my eyes adjust ...

there's some faint light from the skylight windows high above me.

But a chill wind blows through under the bare floorboards.

Suddenly, I can feel a presence – a brooding, malevolent presence somewhere in the far corner of the room. I can hear its laboured breathing ...

Smell its bristling excitement.

I swallow hard.

I want to say something, find words to explain my being there, but my throat's dried out and the words won't form. I get the feeling this thing's not in the mood for listening anyway.

(Boom)

I sense it move towards me.

It's ...

It's ...

(Boom)

It's like it's void of light, absorbing – not reflecting – what little there is.

A dark shape stalking me.

I can't move. I ...

can't.

It's a ...

(Boom)

beast, but one that moves like a man and is shaped like a man.

Maybe an enlarged head.

(Boom)

Definitely an enlarged head.

It's closer. Oh God. I can taste its breath now …

(gag)

a foul vapour filling my nose and throat. Then its …

great hands fall on my shoulders and its mis-shaped head obscures the remaining light from the window.

Oh God.

(gag)

It's touching me.

Caressing me.

Touching and stroking my face, my hair, my mouth.

(gag)

I c-c-c-can't m-m-m-moooovvve.

H-h-h-help m-me.

H-h-help.

H-h ...

'Get the fuck off of me!'

I get my foot under it and grab its neck and push it over my head.

I've got to get away from this thing.

I've got to get away from it.

It whines piteously ...

And ...

I'm screaming at it

Enraged, I

Fly at it

locking my arm around its great fucking bull-neck and wrestle the fucker to the ground.

It's pinned beneath me, **huffing** and **puffing** and ready to **erupt**, but I'm going to hold on ...

I'm going to hold on ...

I'm going to keep pressing it to the floor, even if it ...

Thump.

It's fucking thrown me off ...

... I'm ...

... across the room into another corner.

Where did it go?

Where is it?

Then I can see it. (gag)

Climbing the walls like a great spider (gag) ready to launch itself at me again. I back against the wall, sidling my way (gag) towards the window.

I'll fucking jump through it and fall below rather than face this (gag) … this creature again.

I fucking will.

I will.

I …

The wall behind me gives way.

It's another door.

As one door closes another one always opens. That's what my Mum used to say.

I find myself in a narrow winding staircase in the tower of the building.

My heart's beating like **BOOM-BIDI-BOOM-BIDI-BOOM** now, like someone hammering my chest from the inside.

I know this fucking thing's at my heels, so no loitering here …

Oh no.

I spring up the stone steps three, four at a time, bounding up

Up

Up

to the apex of this …

tower.

It's a tower.

I'm in a tower.

Stop.

Stagger.

Gasp for breath. (gag)

Another door.

Another fucking door.

Would you fucking believe it.

But different.

A rough, wooden door with iron fixings. Behind it …

A woman weeping.

I beat the door and beg her to let me in, let me help her. I feel like I'm a prisoner, but maybe, just maybe, together, we can find a way out of here. I just feel it.

'C'mon! Open up!'

I'm beating this door as loud as I can, but she just keeps on weeping.

Maybe she can't hear me above the sound of her own tears, or maybe she's locked in and can't move.

I listen at the door, trying to control my own breathing.

'Can you hear me?'

A pause. The crying stops.

'In there. Can you hear me?'

Footsteps approach the door between us.

'Can you hear me?'

'I can hear you.'

'I want to help.'

'You can't help. There's nothing you can do.'

Her voice is ... odd. Echoey. Like it's double tracked, recorded. Shaky. Crackly.

'Are you alright?'

She laughed. She actually laughed. The door swung open.

I hesitate. I don't know anything anymore. I don't know if I'm brave enough to go in there. I'm scared of what's in there.

I stand on this side and push back the heavy partition to reveal the room. She's standing on the arched window ledge, framed by light from outside. I can hear a crowd ... a mob ... chanting. She's wearing a ragged scarecrow wedding dress, torn, and matted with blood and dirt. Her back's to me and her long tousled hair falls down behind her. She's wearing a crown, some sort of tarnished tiara, this skinny ... emaciated girl ... and ... she looks like she's ready to jump. I don't know what to do. It's a small circular room, littered with dolls, all broken and filthy and ruined. If I make it across and try to save her …

I might …

I can't save her. I don't want to. I can't. I'm too scared.

She turns and looks at me. Anorexia Nervosa … then she …

she lets out some horrific high-pitched whine – a single, deafening note that sustains and grows till it hurts my ears. It's inhuman, impossible, like something electronic, but it just keeps building and building until I think my ears are going to bleed and my head is going to burst.

'STOP IT!!!' I scream and …

She dives out of the window. The noise stops and I run to the window. Below, all the masked revellers from the soiree in the entrance hall stand there in a seething mass, some with lit torches, then nearer the middle, lighted candles, with those in the very centre without fire but hands upturned ready to catch the falling maid. She lands in their arms, her arms outstretched, legs together, falling perfectly into their crucifix shape. They cheer and carry her off down the hill, baying in triumph, but I know she is gone. Dead.

Gone.

I turn round. There are cradles in the room – dozens of them. Hundreds maybe. Wretched, broken cradles lying in heaps, one on top of another, like firewood but with a few tattered wisps of dirty white lace sticking out at odd bits. In between are the gnarled remains of Moses baskets. Where are all the babies? Where did they all …

(Boom)

Beating behind me. There, in the doorway, the dark beast.

(Boom)

It lunges at me but I jump to the side and it flies out of the window. I hear it, as it falls –

down

down

down

Then I run.

I fly down the stairs rolling off the walls, and stumbling, falling

downwards

downwards

downward

down

down

down

until …

I stop. It's another corridor.

I'm okay.

I'm alright.

Everything is calm again.

I'm calm again.

This corridor is different. It seems almost … modern.

Roughcast concrete walls. Strip lighting, illuminating everything in front of me. The only darkness is in the passage from where I came. I listen. I can't hear a thing.

Nothing chasing me. I'm alone again.

I walk down the corridor.

I only want to get out of place now. I've had enough.

This passageway is windowless, but it feels … underground.

For some reason.

It also feels as though the storm had passed.

Somehow …

I know …

I feel …

it's going to be okay.

This passage winds round and round and round

but it feels okay.

Right somehow.

I'm not going into the bowels of the place, but rather closer to its centre.

Yes. I'm sure I'm moving closer to its centre.

I come to another door. This is the end. There's nowhere else to go except back the way I came.

And that's not really an option.

A panelled, wooden door painted in white gloss going yellow. A Bakelite knob two thirds of the way up it, level with my chest. It opens easily.

Inside, steps lead down to a basement lit by a

solitary electric light bulb hanging from the middle of the ceiling. The room's full of shelving, floor to ceiling, around the walls, with massive gun metal cases containing what appear to be hundreds of thousands of small grey metal drawers all covered in dust. Each drawer is marked with a little white card in a little metal holder. There's something really old fashioned about it, like something begun many years before, but now in a state of neglect. I can't think what it reminds me of ... can't quite bring it to mind. So I step down into this vast room and it strikes me. What it is. It's like a large library indexing system. A vault.

Records are kept here.

A little man steps out from behind one of the shelf units. He's short and squat, wearing highly polished yet dusty shoes, and a black uniform over a starched white shirt and black tie. He also has a peaked cap with a ribbon around it – at the front is a little badge with the word *Curator* on it.

'Who are you?' I ask.

'I'm the Curator,' he replies.

Fair enough. Ask a silly question.

We stand there for a moment.

He's watching me, not indifferently, not expectantly, but simply as if he's waiting for the next question. He doesn't seem to be in any hurry, but just ... ready.

I look at him. His face is a little puffy and middle aged, his skin ruddy and slightly pock-marked, and his nose is a bit of a bulbous snout. He's still staring at me, but not at my eyes, rather keeping his gaze at his own eye level, somewhere around my chest. His hands are behind his back and he's ... or seems to be ... rocking back and forth on his heels – just ever so slightly, almost imperceptibly. He doesn't seem in the least surprised by my presence, just content to be waiting.

Funny.

I feel like I could stand here for quite a while, but

decide I should say something.

'I ...'

then couldn't think what to say. The little man just keeps looking at my chest. Occasionally he blinks. His eyelashes are metal grey, as is what I can see of his hair, which is slicked back with hair oil.

'I ... erm ... ' I try again. But there seems to be nothing to say. I think about explaining how I came to be here ... or maybe what's happened to me in this house, but I get a strong feeling he doesn't really care.

We stand there for a wee while longer and I realise it's pretty unimportant to me too now.

'Would you like to see the files?' he asks me, his voice neutral, eyes still looking towards my chest.

I realise he isn't really looking at me, but staring into middle distance and my chest just happens to be in the way. I test this out by stepping to the side, but he blinks and re-focuses on my chest. So much for that theory.

'Do you want to see the files?' he asks again, a touch more insistently this time.

'Erm ... yes,' I say, not really sure what to say. What files?

'This way.' He beckons me with a small crook of his finger as he turns his back and leads the way through the shelving.

As he starts off through the passage, I re-assess the room. It might be even bigger than I first thought. It's definitely underground, so it could cover an area much, much bigger than the house. Whatever that is. In fact, this could be much, much bigger. And there's not an inch of space wasted. The units are seven feet high and three feet thick, each set perpendicular to the wall with just enough room to walk between each. In fact, walking from one end to the other, you're forced to slalom around the jutting edge of the units, weaving between the corner of the facing units. It's like tracing the path through the teeth of a giant zip fastener and this little man, the Curator, despite a rather large midriff, does this with practiced assurance and some aplomb. His wee, short legs and brisk, quick steps are obviously well suited to the task.

Suddenly, without warning, he turns into a dark alley created by two of the long shelf cases and walks right up the end. I hesitate where I am, lingering at the edge of the shelf. It's dark. In fact the light's so dim I can hardly make him out. In fact he's disappeared.

Then there's a scraping sound on the tiled floor and a little overhead light comes on above where he's standing. He's perched on a small set of steps about three feet high with a long pole at one side to help balance. The pole is bigger than him, even standing on the top step. He pauses for a moment, with a trace of impatience, as he waits for me to follow him down. Something at the back of my mind is starting to nag, a small alarm telling me not to go down there.

He drums his fingers on the shelf and beckons me with his finger once more. I have to go.

As I approach, the poor lighting and converging walls have the effect of making him seem to grow larger.

Hmm. I shake my head and blink a few times to wipe this impression.

'Okay?' I ask as I arrive next to him. I realise he only appeared bigger because he was standing on the stepladder. He is about two and a half feet taller than me now.

He doesn't reply, but steps down from the stepladder and stands back on the floor. He looks at me again, back to focusing on my chest

I stand for a moment, unsure what to do next.

He gives a brief cough and gestures for me to climb the steps. I notice one of the drawers is protruding slightly. He gestures again, looking me straight in the eye for the first time and flicking his eyebrows towards the open drawer. His eyes are warm but still hard. He's not forcing me … but … I don't feel I can refuse him either. I climb the steps.

The overhead light is clipped to one of the higher shelves, making it possible to read some of the index cards on the drawer fronts. Those above the open drawer are:

```
Ideas (untried); Ideas (discarded);
        Ignorances (displayed);
         Impulses (repressed);
      Innovations (thwarted)
```

I look back at the Curator. He was examining his fingernails. I don't like this.

Other titles can be discerned in the narrow light –

```
        Loves (unrequited);
      Moments (squandered);
         Omens (ignored);
Poems (unwritten); Prayers (unspoken);
      Promises (broken)
```

Suddenly I'm trembling. I don't like this at all. I'm not sure about this. I …

tip up the front of the open drawer. Its card reads:

```
        Letters (dead)
```

Oh fuck.

Oh God.

I nearly fall off the steps. Behind me, I feel the stubby hands of the Curator catch me and balance me back on the steps. My hands are shaking. My whole body's trembling. I'm not in control here. It's like my body is a robot and, unbidden, I'm rifling through the cards in the drawer. A tiny, contracting spot on my brain is screaming at me not to do this. But my robot arms pull one out. It reads:

Dear Dad,
*   You should see what I can see. There's*
nothing, literally nothing between me and deep space.
*   I could fall off the world and nobody would*
ever know. It might happen. It might happen. That's
why I wanted to . . .

I throw it on the floor. The Curator tuts and I can hear him
bending down to pick it up. I pull another one out:

Dear Mum,
*   What's happened to me? What have I*
become? I don't even know who I am any more. I
don't even know who I am.

Another:

Dear Fiona,
*   By the time you read this I'll have gone. It's*
best you don't know where, though I couldn't tell you
even if I wanted to because . . . I don't even know
myself.

On no. This is too much.
        Too too much.
        No.
        I fall onto the floor. It's dirty and dusty. Tears prick
my eyes. I look up at the little man, hold out the letter.
        'What is this? WHAT IS THIS!!??'
        He coughs and rolls his eyes upwards, like he
doesn't like my tone of voice. He puckers his lips and checks
his wristwatch. Then he looks at me again.
        'I'm sorry,' I'm sobbing. 'I'm sorry.'
        He purses his lips and arches his eyebrows.
        'Please tell me.' I'm weeping, I'm howling, I'm
crying my eyes out. 'Please.'

'You know,' he says.
I …
I …
can't..
stop …
c …
c …
crying.

I wipe my nose on my sleeve.
'I … I … I suppose I'm lucky.'
He smiles. Not enough to show his teeth, but a smile nevertheless. There was a look on his face. Something almost like … sympathy? Pity? Amusement?
He beckons me with that little crook of his finger again and marches off down the passage. I follow, toppling the contents of the drawer all over the floor and stumbling into the shelves as I go, sobbing and blinded by tears.

43: DEAR ME

I'm lucky.

I'm sitting on the top of this hill watching the sun come up.

It's beautiful.

It's stopped raining.

Everything is damp. Everything is wet.

But it's stopped raining.

A rainbow sunrise.

It's beautiful. The sun's breathing out colour into the landscape. To the South I can see the city, its mazy features outlined by street lamps, once proud in the cover of the night, now cowering and wan in the majesty of true, natural light.

To the West, just a few yards away, I can see it. Home.

Time to go.

Time to go home.

I start running.

If I hurry up I'll catch Mum before she goes to work and she might make me some porridge.

I run faster.

If I see Dad I'll talk to him. Just wish him good morning.

On my own street now.

If I see Christina I'll …

There it is. My house.

Listen!

Bird song!

I'm so sorry.

I'm so sorry for everything.

I'll make it up. I'll make it right.

I'll tell Mum I'm sorry.

I'll give her a hug.

I'll tell Dad I'm sorry.

I'll give him a hug.

I'll tell him I love him.

I'll buy Christina some sweets and give her a hug and tell her I love her.

Hell!

I'll even give Steven a hug!

My street.

God! It's beautiful! It's so beautiful.

I …

I thought …

I thought …

I thought I was never going to see it again.

Right.

C'mon now.

Stop blubbing.

No crying. Get a grip here.

Pull yourself together.

God! There's Mr Melrose's house! He's painted that smelly old pigeon loft. Not before time.

Where …

did all these cars come from? There's hundreds of them.

Must be a wedding.

Or a funeral.

Hey! There's Mrs McAllister. Always first in the queue when the Co-op opens.

'Hi!' I greet her.

I want to give her a hug.

She pulls her coat up and her headscarf down and beetles past me without a word.

Fair enough.

Cars …

Dozens of them.

A hearse.

Outside.

My house.

The front door opens.

Pallbearers bring out a brown teak coffin.

With brass handles.

A short fat man with metallic grey hair slicked back under a top hat with a fluttering black chiffon ribbon around it. And a black top coat. And black polished shoes. And a bulbous snout nose. And pock marked skin. He looks straight ahead.

Unblinking.

Unmoved.

Doing his job.

Dad walks out behind him.

Thinner, greyer.

Older.

Dad.

Dad in a black Crombie and a black tie.

Then Steven.

Fatter, greyer.

Older.

Steven.

Steven in a black Crombie and a black tie.

Comforting ...

Christina.

Fatter.

No older.

Swaddled in black.

Sobbing into Steven's side.

Sobbing and wailing ...

Grieving.

Who for?

The coffin passes me ...

Dad holds the gate open for Steven and Christina.

They walk through.

I walk up to Dad.

He looks straight through me.

'Dad?' (don't cry)

'Dad?' (don't ...)

'Dad ... where's Mum? Where is she? What's happened to her? Who's in the coffin? (stop blubbing. Stop it.) 'Who's in the coffin?'

He walks right past me.

Follows Steven.

Follows the coffin.

Wearied.

Beaten.

'Wait ...' They're all ignoring me. 'Can't you hear me? Wait ...'

The wee Chief Pallbearer holds open the door of the limousine behind the hearse. Steven enters. Then Christina. Then Dad. (There will be a day ...)

The coffin is laid in the back of the hearse.

There are flowers on top of the coffin. (... when everyone you knew ...)

The Chief Pallbearer continues to hold open the door of the limo.

I stumble towards him.

(... and everyone who knew you ...)

There's snot and tears running down my face.

Half of my teeth are missing and my breath tastes sour.

My feet are rotting inside my crumbling shoes.

My crotch feels sore and sweaty.

My clothes are filthy and threadbare.

This dead man's overcoat feels like it's sopped up all the dirty rainwater like a sponge.

I know I smell – pungent. Noxious.

Like I'm rotting away.

My legs won't hold me up. They just give way.

I'm slumped against this tree just ...

rotting away.

Still the Chief Pallbearer waits at the door of the limousine.

He must be waiting for me.

I try to get up. I want to, I really do.

But I can't.

I'm just …

too tired.

Exhausted.

He touches the brim of his top hat, saluting. Then he closes the door.

And they drive away.

And I'm left …

I feel like my head's sinking into this tree

This tree …

outside our house …

I can hardly see …

It's getting dark …

The sun's setting again …

It's … setting again?

The car drives away …

Into the sun.
Set.
My fingers fall into the soil.
I can feel the tree roots.
They're creeping like tentacles … around me
My fingers …
going deeper …
becoming …
roots …
my legs …
my arms …
my body …

being …
absorbed …
inhaled …
by this …
tree.

He turns and looks at me. The chiffon ribbon is fluttering behind him in the wind. He says:

'One day, everyone you knew and everyone who knew you will be dead. Nobody alive will know what you looked like. Nobody who will know your name. Nobody will care about you or anything you knew about.'

I recognise him now …

'Then you'll be dead,' he said.

'Then you'll be dead.'

Publishing May 2001

The Dark Ship
Anne MacLeod
This vast literary saga celebrates love, music and poetry in a finely woven story that reflects the complex past of a community on a Scottish island.
1-903238-27-7
£9.99

Dead Letter House
Drew Campbell
Suspend your disbelief for a bizarre trip into the surreal. On a twenty mile walk home a young man explores time and space and discovers his own heaven and hell.
1-903238-29-3
£7.99

The Gravy Star
Hamish MacDonald
One man's hike from post-industrial urban sprawl to lost love and a burnt-out rural idyll.
'A moving and often funny portrait ... of the profound relationship between Glasgow and the wild land to its north.' James Robertson,
1-903238-26-9   author of *The Fanatic*.
£9.99

Strange Faith
Graeme Williamson
This haunting novel tells the story of a young man torn between past allegiances and the promise of a new life.
'Calmly compelling, strangely engaging.' Dilys Rose
1-903238-28-5
£9.99

About 11:9

Supported by the Scottish Arts Council National Lottery Fund and partnership funding, 11:9 publish the work of writers both unknown and established, living and working in Scotland or from a Scottish background. 11:9's brief is to publish contemporary literary novels, and is actively searching for new talent. If you wish to submit work send an introductory letter, a brief synopsis of your novel, a biographical note about yourself and two typed sample chapters to: Editorial Administrator, 11:9, Neil Wilson Publishing Ltd, Suite 303a, The Pentagon Centre, 36 Washington Street, Glasgow, G3 8AZ. Details are also available from our website at **www.11-9.co.uk.**

If you would like to be added to a mailing list about future publications, either register on our website or send your name and address to 11:9, Neil Wilson Publishing Ltd, Suite 303a, The Pentagon Centre, 36 Washington Street, Glasgow, G3 8AZ.

11:9 refers to 11 September 1997 when the Scottish people voted to re-establish their parliament in Edinburgh.